WILSON'S WALL

WILSON'S WALL

ALBERT RUGGIERO

TATE PUBLISHING
AND ENTERPRISES, LLC

Published by Tate Publishing & Enterprises, LLC
127 E. Trade Center Terrace | Mustang, Oklahoma 73064 USA
1.888.361.9473 | www.tatepublishing.com

Tate Publishing is committed to excellence in the publishing industry. The company reflects the philosophy established by the founders, based on Psalm 68:11,
"The Lord gave the word and great was the company of those who published it."

Published in the United States of America

ISBN: 978-1-68187-397-8
1. Fiction / General
2. Fiction / Romance / Historical / General
15.08.13

Canst thou not minister to a mind diseased,
Pluck from the memory a rooted sorrow,
Raze out the written troubles of the brain
And with some sweet oblivious antidote
Cleanse the stuffed bosom of that perilous stuff
Which weighs upon the heart?

—Macbeth

Contents

1

SQUEEZE THE UNIVERSE INTO A BALL

IN RICHMOND, VIRGINIA, the capital thrived during the war, then starved, then burned. But in the North, there was such abundance that the construction of the Capitol dome didn't stop even during the war. Washington grew, then got fatter, then glowed with promise. The gaunt Jefferson Davis fled his capitol; the bearded Lincoln was assassinated in his. No bombs fell on the northern cities or the rural farms. Despite that, the devastation that was evident was in the maiming of its children limping back from war. These were the times that these people lived in, worked in, and died in.

Lawrence, the taller of the two, and Burton, his former sergeant, rode a buckboard up the dusty Connecticut road toward a two-story clapboard farm house. The dust made them bury their chins in their chests. Lawrence grabbed at the July 20, 1865 copy of the *Hartford Courant* from under the seat to cover his face. It was slippery in his hands. And he smiled at the headline. The headline read: "Courant Extra! Glorious News! The End of the War. Let the People Rejoice."

Lawrence had the reins and snapped them over the horse's rump. It trotted faster up the rise.

"Whoa!" Lawrence shouted. A minute later, he pulled back on the reins, then placed the reins on his lap while he opened and closed his fingers to get the circulation back in them. He stopped the buckboard at the crest of the hill, directly in front of a white two-story clapboard farmhouse with green shutters. The horse neighed and stamped its hoof. Three Boston pine rocking chairs bowed to them from the porch while they rocked in the summer wind. "Isn't it beautiful?" he asked as he spread out his arms in front of himself, followed by him tightly grabbing the seat.

"Wait here. I'll be right back," Lawrence said. He slowly let himself down, with a painful groan, while the seat squeaked as he got off. He favored his right foot, dragging his left a little and grimacing with pain as he walked toward the back of the house and in the direction of the summer kitchen. Walking toward the house, he smiled as he glanced to his left.

There, under the oak tree was the root cellar where Abigail and him spent many hours reading and talking about the Greek heroes in the *Iliad*. It was built into the ground with a heavy slatted wooden door at the entrance. Brambles had grown up and over the roof; grape vines wrapped themselves around the white picket fence that surrounded the little building. He was thirteen then and Abigail was only nine. In his memory, he could still smell the earthy odor of the cellar and the sweet aroma of the apples that were stored in the corner.

At three o'clock, the sun blazed through the humid New England air, making the sweat drip down from under his Union cap.

When he reached the kitchen door, he saw Abigail pick up a brown crusted mince pie in her white apron. She had dark shoulder-length hair parted in the middle and wore a crinoline bell-shaped dress with loose frilled sleeves to the wrists. He hadn't seen his stepsister in a dress in a long time, so he stared at the petite young lady, and at that instant, didn't recognize her. The last time he saw her, before he left for the army, she was only thirteen and he was eighteen.

She turned toward the door and screamed, letting go of the pie so it fell all over the wooden floor with the metal pie plate echoing through the kitchen.

"I'm sorry. I didn't mean to frighten you," he said. He realized that he was standing at attention but relaxed from his old discipline as soon as she started to talk.

"Yes, can I help you?" She warily walked toward the door, looking down trying to avoid the pieces of pie smashed all over the floor. Her little feet shuffled closer to the stranger.

"Abigail, it's me, Lawrence." He put his hands under his chin as if he were a young schoolgirl. The savory aroma of the just baked pie followed her out the door.

From the expression on her face, Lawrence realized that she wasn't seeing the boy who went to war many years ago. She was looking at a man that was tempered and hardened by his experiences. Her blue eyes lit up when she recognized who it was and in an instant threw her arms around his neck.

"Oh my god! I can't believe it's really you," she said.

He held her close to his chest, as her legs dangled just above the floor. Her hair was silky smooth against his cheek. The last human being he embraced was a dying soldier. After a while, his heart stopped but the thump of hers was strong and alive. Tears welled up in his eyes when he thought of the difference. After he let her down, she looked up at him, covering her eyes from the sun.

"We weren't expecting you until tomorrow," she said.

"We traveled with a lantern in front of the horse and by the light of the full moon."

Lawrence smelled a vanilla and lemon perfume emanating from Abigail. She was the most beautiful thing he had seen in a long time. Her dark skin contrasted by her blue eyes drew him down like a magnet. Pale-to-fair skin was considered attractive, a sign of social standing. But she was a young working girl, and her face had been kissed brown by the sun.

When he bent down a second time to kiss her, he felt himself being lifted up from behind. Noah Wilson, his stepfather, came up behind him and lifted him into the air. He saw sun-tanned muscular hands grab him under his ribs and bounce him so hard that he slid off his feet and landed on his rump. After that, his ribs ached.

"Lawrence, you old son of a gun. Good to see ya again," he shouted. Noah was a small but muscular man dressed in a double-breasted, blue pullover shirt, trousers with a pair of suspenders holding them up, and a wide-brimmed, yellow straw hat.

Noah reached down and offered the young man his beefy hand. Lawrence reached for his hand, and before he knew it, he was pulled up to a standing position. And Lawrence could feel the tenderness in his vice-like grip.

"I can't believe I'm home," he said, looking around first at the house and then at Noah and Abigail. Noah had an earthy smell about him as if he'd just come from the field.

"Well, ya are," Noah said. "An' dis time you're goin' to stay right here where you belong. You an' your friend get washed up at the pump. Abby an' me will rustle up some vittles for ya." They both went into the kitchen, but Noah strode into the little structure as if he was going to plow up the guts of the building.

Lawrence motioned to Burton to come up to the pump. Burton reined the horse to a steel ring on a granite pillar in the front yard and walked toward him with his bedroll tucked under his arm and a white burlap bag slung over his shoulder. When Lawrence stepped off the porch, Abigail grabbed the striker hanging on the wrought iron triangle dinner bell and bounced and rolled the wand inside of it. The ringing—kind of like the bell on a locomotive, only louder—could be heard far and wide.

Lawrence turned and asked, "What's that for? We know it's time to eat."

"It's for Daniel Washington, our other farm hand. He should be coming in from the field any minute now," she said as she stretched her neck looking past the barn and into the pasture.

When the two men were at last at the pump, they removed their shirts. Lawrence was a thin, bony rib-exposed dog, while Burton was overfed and a barrel-chested bear. They reveled in splashing each other and putting their faces under the blue crystal stream of water. Under other circumstances, these animals would have been enemies, slashing at each other and showing their teeth, but for now, they were friends. Each gush of liquid washed away the heat and dust of the day. Before he went to the house, he reached down deep into his pocket and pulled out a round light-brown pill about double the size of a pea and popped it into his mouth. It was an opium pill, and when the pain from his foot got to the point where he couldn't stand it anymore, he would eat another one.

Lawrence looked back at the house and noticed Abigail and Noah staring at him from the porch. Abigail put her hand to her mouth and then gazed at the ground, not able to keep her eyes on the emaciated soldier. Noah just took off his straw hat, shook his head, and went back into the kitchen.

Fifteen minutes later, they all sat at a pine table in the summer kitchen; Abigail, her father, Lawrence, Burton, and Daniel. Daniel was the unexpected guest who was already sitting at the table when the two soldiers came in. He sat in silence with his hands folded on his lap and his back straight and tall against the back of the chair. He was forty, with grey streaks of age on the side of his short hair, watchful brown eyes, and a light brown Negro completion, only one shade darker than Abigail's sun-tanned face. He twisted a bit in his overalls, anticipating the meal.

It was a single room building, perfectly rectangular, that had mason jars lining the floor filled with preserved fruit, vegetables, and pickles. A zinc sink and an icebox occupied the other side of the room. Under one of the windows was a wood-fired stove that attached to the brick chimney outside. The smolder embers filled the room with a homey atmosphere.

"Who's this Abby?" Lawrence asked.

"Oh, I should have introduced everybody," she said apologetically. "This is Daniel Washington. He's been with us for how long now?" She turned to him, her voice trying to be formal and proper.

"Started here in sixty-one or the beginning of sixty-two, miss. I think," Daniel said.

"Pleased to meet you, Dan. Okay if I call you Dan?" Lawrence asked as he got up and shook his hand.

"Sure. No problem."

"Been since sixty-one, Daniel. Almost four years. I dun know what I would've done without you," Noah said.

"Daniel, this is Burton," Abigail said. She gestured to him with an open palm.

"Pleased to make your acquaintance, sir." Daniel extended his hand in friendship. His hand floated in space for a long time until he realized that there was no handshake coming. So he pulled his hand back little by little and rested it on the table.

Burton's mouth tightened and he frowned. He leaned forward as if to attack him. After that, he scanned Daniel from head to foot in defiance of his presence. Then with contempt, he lowered his eyebrows and turned away, as if he were not worth looking at, followed by him pulling out his gun and putting it next to his plate.

"I don't shake hands with slaves," he said while pushing back on his chair.

Noah rested his elbows on the table and looked in Burton's direction. "Daniel's no slave, he's a free man. Slavery was got rid of in Connecticut in forty-eight," he said.

"It's okay, Mr. Wilson, I'd feel better eatin' on the steps of the porch, if you don't mind," he said.

"Okay, Daniel. If that's how ya feel about it," Noah said. "Abby, make a plate for Daniel, would ya?"

"All right, Pa," she said. Then she put a chicken leg on a plate with a pile of roasted potatoes next to it. She handed it to him. There was an unbearable silence in the room. The last sounds were the scrape of the chair being slid out from under the table, the shuffle of him walking across the wood floor, and the shutting of the door behind him as he left.

Lawrence suddenly got up and skipped along on his good foot. Then he went over to what was left of the mince pie that had fallen on the floor. It sat in a bowl on the counter. He pushed the broken pieces onto his spoon and then into his mouth. He smiled and closed his eyes savoring every bite. "I can't tell you how long it's been since I had a piece of mince pie. I'd forgotten the taste of cinnamon and cloves. I just couldn't let it go to waste," he said.

"But Lawrence that was on the—"

"Abby!" Noah said.

"What, Dad?"

"It's all right. Let it go," he whispered.

She smiled ever so softly at her father and then turned back toward Lawrence. "Are you still reading like we use to do in the root cellar?" Abigail asked.

"Sure am," he said. "Those were peaceful happy times, Abby." She grinned and then blushed as he stumbled back to the table.

Meanwhile Burton took off his gun belt and laid it on the table next to him, moving the pail of cold milk aside. Then he propped up the white canvas bag close to his chair.

The steam from the just roasted chicken and potatoes floated in front of Lawrence and Burton. They could hardly contain themselves; the food smelled so good. It brought back memories of home.

Lawrence's left foot rested alongside of the table pointing toward Abby. She frowned as she stared at it and then looked into his eyes.

"I know I should've written you about this," Lawrence said, pointing at his foot with his fork. "I didn't want to worry you."

"What did they do to you? Those dam rebs, I've got half a mind to join up myself and teach 'em all a lesson they'd never forget!"

"No, Abby, it wasn't Johnny Reb that did this to me. I got it when a caisson knocked me over and then rolled over my ankle. They patched me up and put me behind the desk because I could read and write. How many times I would sit and talk and exchange tobacco with them, before the accident, when there was a break in the fighting. They're just like us, only on a different side. After we were done chawing our tobacco, we would get up, go back to our own lines, and carry on killing each other."

Abigail grabbed his arm to make a point. "See, I told you reading the *McGuffey Reader*, the *Iliad*, and the Bible would save your soul."

"I don't know about those books saving my soul, but they sure enough saved my life. Pushing the pen was a whole lot better than pulling the trigger." They both chuckled. Burton shot a look at Lawrence.

"Yeah, I was the guy that pushed those men to pull those triggers," Burton said. "Let's eat!" He banged his fork and knife on the table.

Abigail got up and walked over to the cast-iron stove and took off a large steaming coffee pot and placed it in the center of the table. She had four cloth napkins under her arm, placing one in front of each man. "Now, you men, use those."

Noah took the cloth napkin whipped it open and stuffed it under his chin. "Now, boys, help yourself. What you can't reach yell for."

In the middle of all the clattering of dishes and the passing of food, Abby with refinement wiped her mouth and addressed the sergeant. "Mr. Goldsborough, Lawrence wrote us that you've been in the army all your life."

"Yep, sure have." A piece of chicken hung off of his short beard as he talked. "Well, I'll tell you, honey, I've been in the army since I was a kid. Recruits don't listen to you anymore. I get no respect. That's why I got out." He talked through a mouthful of food. "I came from a small farm in Illinois, but the only home I ever knew was in the army. Thought I'd try civilian life for a change."

"I see," Abby said.

"You don't have to be so formal, honey," Burton said, and then he reached over and caressed her hand and winked at her.

Abigail pulled her hand away and held it on her lap as if Burton had contaminated her.

Lawrence saw what had happened. He was angry and clenched his jaw and leaned his elbows closer over his plate and stared at Burton, but Burton was too busy eating to notice. He was going to push the issue, although for now he felt it was better left alone. *Maybe it was Abigail's nervousness that caused the incident*, he thought.

"Does anybody want another cup of coffee?" she asked. She stood up without warning. And with trembling hands, she picked up the large coffee pot in the center of the table.

On purpose, she overfilled Burton's cup with the scalding coffee so it spilled into his lap. He got up fast, grabbing his gun and using the napkin to wipe off the coffee on his pants.

"Abby!" Lawrence backed away from the coffee spilling over the edge of the table.

"I'm sorry. Is everybody all right?" She stood still, frozen by the men's stares, until finally she began to cry. She slammed the heavy pot back on the table and ran out the door.

"Excitable young lady, isn't she?" Burton said. He sat back down and continued eating with gusto.

Lawrence turned to Noah. "What's wrong with Abigail?" he asked.

"She's jus' upset about spillin' the coffee. She wanted everything to be jus' right for when ya came home."

"No, it's more than that," he said.

"Whatda you mean?" Noah asked.

"It's something I have to take care of. Don't worry about it." The young soldier swung his bad foot over as he backed the chair away from the table. Then he hobbled out the door.

Daniel was sitting on the steps of the porch when Lawrence came out of the door.

"Danny, did you see where Abigail went?" he asked.

"Yep. She ran into the barn. She seemed mighty upset."

"Thanks."

2

ABIGAIL'S DILEMMA

ABIGAIL FLOPPED DOWN on a bale of hay and stared out toward the field of asparagus. Their purple hairlike tops waved in the wind. Lawrence limped into the barn door as a cloud of dust trailed behind him. The smell of new-mown hay filled the building and the earthy pungent aroma of ripe apples hung in the air. But Lawrence had a sick bitter expression on his face. He limped over and sat next to her on the bale of hay.

"Abby, tell me what's wrong."

"I don't want to talk about it," she said. "Tell me about the war."

"That's something I don't want to talk about, that's for sure."

She held his hands—hands that were calloused and bony. "Wasn't it exciting and noble like we read about in the *Iliad*?" She searched his eyes for an answer, but all she saw was a peculiar blank expression on his face. His eyes widened and he began to sweat. "Lawrence, what's happening?"

He became quiet and a peculiar frightened stare filled his eyes. He pushed his cap back on his head, revealing his curly black hair. "The gods didn't protect us. They didn't even care." Sweat beaded all over his face at the same time that he put his index finger up to his mouth. "Quiet, do you hear them bombarding?"

"No, I don't." Something powerful began to suck him away from her. In desperation, she pulled him close to her chest. On impulse, she cradled him next to her heartbeat. "It's all right. There's no guns here, no bombs," she said.

There was a familiar scent of vanilla coming from her neck that enveloped them in a loving cocoon. She had always just been his stepsister and nothing more, but now she saw herself as a woman.

He suddenly sat up and blankly stared out the barn door. He grabbed a handful of hay and it rustled in his hand, then he glanced back at her for a second. "I'll tell you some of what happened, but after that, I don't want to talk about it again."

"Okay," she said.

"There were no heroes like we read about, there were just survivors." He tossed the hay in his hand across the barn. "There were just blood and severed limbs, smoke and the stench of rotting bodies. Some of my job was to record the casualties in the field, and from what I saw, it was a terrible waste of human life." He let out a long sigh. "For days, the smoke from the rifles would settle into the valleys. Looking out over the hills gave you the impression of being in the clouds high above all the killing and wars, like you were an angel, but I felt like a devil because I couldn't do anything to change it. But for me, the worst thing was seeing the men not having enough to eat, not as much our boys, but those rebs were like walking skeletons." He laughed and shook his head. "Have you ever been hungry, Abby? I don't mean just ready for supper. I mean ready to eat the bark off the trees, that kind of hungry?"

"No, can't say as I have."

"Well, I've seen people that were that hungry, and there was nothing I could do about it. Now, it's all I think about."

"Lawrence, please, I don't want to hear anymore. I'm sorry I asked. You only have to think about the farm and me now, all right?" He flinched when she wrapped her arms around his waist. She waited till he relaxed and then rested her head on his shoulder. His collarbone dug into her cheek. They stayed that way for a long time until Abby broke the silence.

She sat up and lightly put her hand on his shoulder. "I understand. But you're home now." As a final point, she got up, walked a few paces, and then turned around. "The farm will heal you," she said. "You'll be in a place where things are alive and growing. No more death, no more hunger."

She thought, *Maybe the farm would be his salvation. Maybe the living present will wipe out his memories of death in the past.* She looked at Lawrence, fighting back his tears as they welled up in his eyes; she nodded her head not saying a word. But from that day on, she saw herself as a woman to be pursued. And all those images of her in pigtails dissolved away.

"Come on, I'll show you your room." She grabbed Lawrence's hands, and a young woman's excitement welled up in her chest. They headed back toward the house. The couple passed through the kitchen on their way upstairs, and Lawrence did his best to keep up with Abigail. "Pa, I'm going to show Lawrence his room." Abigail pulled him along as they went up the stairs and into the room that she had maintained all those years. "See, just like you left it."

"Yeah, sure is."

Abigail flopped onto the bed and stared at Lawrence. His green eyes had sadness in them that she hadn't noticed before. She sank deep into the feather mattress and pillow.

He flung his union cap on top of the chest of drawers across from the bed and sat in the straight-backed chair. He took off the neckerchief from around his neck and dipped it in the cool water from the washstand and wiped his face with it. The water dripped down over his sun-tanned face and down onto his chest. "Ahh, that feels good."

After that, Lawrence eased himself on the feather bed next to Abigail. He grabbed her around the waist and pulled her close. They didn't kiss, they just held each other. This wasn't her step brother anymore. It was a man in her bed which made her nervous.

"Do…do you want to see the root cellar?" she asked, while scooting off the bed and standing next to the door.

"Did you keep that place just the same too?" Lawrence asked, smiling at Abby.

"You're making fun of me, and I don't like it." In a snit, she turned her back to him, folding her arms over her chest and talked to the door. "I thought you'd be happy that everything had stayed the same as it was when you were a boy."

Lawrence got up and turned her around and cradled her face in his hands. "Abby, I'm not a little boy anymore."

"I know," she said. Her voice dropped off in disappointment.

This time, he took her hands and pulled her along. "Come on, let's see what you've done." They walked down the stairs and out the front door until they finally stood in front of the root cellar.

"See, just like you left it," Abby said. She opened the little white-washed wooden gate and then Lawrence walked in and pulled open the heavy planked door. They both looked through the open door. In the far left corner was a brown burlap bag of potatoes, a basket of apples, and a wooden carton of peaches. Moisture clung to the fuzzy surface of the peaches so they glistened in the afternoon sun. Two straight-backed chairs occupied the center of the room, and a pile of books sat in the middle of them. Around the edge of the room were garden tools and on the walls hung faded art paintings of Achilles, Hector, and Agamemnon.

Lawrence and Abigail went down the stone stairs into a cool silent room. Lawrence picked up a red apple wiping it off, and then he took a big bite. He winked at Abby. They both sat in the chairs at the same time, looking around, drinking in the peace of their little world. The coolness of the cellar brought back memories to her of their time together. Abigail picked up the *McGuffey Reader* and leafed through the pages. All that could be heard was the scratch and shuffle of the pages being turned.

3

A Sweet Madness

Abigail put down the book and turned to Lawrence. Her eyes were as soft as doves, and Lawrence was mesmerized by their innocence. "Lawrence, kiss me again and again. I can't get enough of your kisses," she said.

He put his left hand under her little head, and with his right hand, he pulled her close. They kissed with vigor as two lips became one. Lawrence's heart beat hard against his chest, and the memory of who he was faded away. They became one writhing, grasping passion.

After that, he pulled her closer so they were sitting together on one chair. "Lie down with me," Lawrence said. They got up and moved the chairs to the back of the root cellar. Lawrence made a bed of burlap bags. "It's not a bed of roses, but it's the best I can do." Suddenly, Lawrence opened the heavy door and went outside. He returned with an orange butterfly weed flower in his hand. He put it on the love bed. "That's better."

"It's beautiful, Lawrence," she said as she picked it up and smelled it. She looked up at him uneasy. "Do you look down on me? Did you know that the city girls look down on me because my complexion is so dark? It's the sun's fault, you know." She smiled.

"I think you're the most beautiful woman in the entire world," he said. "Your cheeks are so lovely and smooth"—he ran the back of his hand gently over her face and touched her hair—"and your black hair is so silky."

"Am I as beautiful as Helen of Troy?" she asked.

"Yes."

Abigail sat on the improvised bed and took Lawrence's hand. She pulled him down next to her. "You're my Achilles in his armor riding over the mountains in his chariot, rushing towards me, anxious to make love to me," she said. "When I hear your voice and see your handsome face, I have to have you next to me."

By now, he was leaning on his elbow nestling close to her side.

"I feel the same way, Abby," he said. "When I see your hair fall across your face and look at your beautiful young mouth and sensuous red lips, I can hardly control myself." Then he unbuttoned her blouse little by little as he watched her. She closed her eyes and breathed with short fits through her pulsing nostrils. Lawrence kissed her eyelids, her cheeks, her long neck, and finally began kissing her twin breasts. They were ripe, smooth, and firm, and their taste made him drunk. Her sweat was a perfume that made his head swim. He wished he could live between her breasts forever, living off her sweet milk. After all, these udders are virgin and their white fluid is ambrosia with magical properties, a delightful liquid. *If I lived there, maybe I could stop hearing the cannons and the screams of the war*, he thought. He could hear a little moan coming from deep in her chest.

She whispered in Lawrence's ear. "Let's take off all our clothes."

Abigail took off her homespun skirt and then her pantalets. Lawrence helped her pull off her Garibaldi-type blouse over her head.

Lawrence took off his trousers and shirt and unfastened his suspenders.

She pushed her thighs toward Lawrence as if she was offering him her young virgin gifts.

It went quick because the passion was boiling up in their chests. As they stripped and fumbled around awkwardly, they kissed and nuzzled each other, trying to keep their lust alive until the time came when they would make love to each other.

This was Lawrence's first love experience, and he did not want to seem unsure or naive, so he orchestrated the movements with a caring hand but with confidence.

Abigail's thighs were round and firm like her breasts, and they invited him to touch them and to travel down with his hand to caress her gorgeous tanned legs; she pulled closer to him when he did that. She continued to kiss his face and nose.

"I love you, Abby," Lawrence said.

"Yes, I love you too. You're my Greek god," she said.

"I'm just a man, not a god."

After that, they both kept silent. They both talked to each other with their hands; caressing, fondling, and petting each other's bodies. Until finally, Lawrence tried to penetrate Abigail, but because she was a virgin, he was unsuccessful. The passion was gone by now and they both lie in each other's arms.

"I'm sorry, Abby," he said.

"It's all right. We can try again when ever we're in the mood," she said. "Let's just stay in each other's arms for now."

At that moment, Lawrence changed his mind about Abigail. Before this, he just thought of her as a young farm girl with not very much insight into how the world worked. But the patience and understanding about their lovemaking made him respect her. It was another aspect of her personality that attracted him to her even more.

Lawrence got up, put his clothes on, grabbed an apple, and started to leave the root cellar.

"Are you all right, Abby?" he asked after he took a bite from the apple. "I have to go up to the barn."

"I'm all right," she said, as she gathered her clothes together and at the same time talked to Lawrence about how happy she was that he was home.

On his way up to the barn, he reached into his pocket and got out one of his opium pills and popped it in his mouth. A minute later, the pain in his foot went away, and by the time he reached the barn, he felt whole again.

4

THE STRAW BED

BY NOW IT was late afternoon and Lawrence had walked up to the barn. He stood at the open door of the building, chomping on an apple and looking at Burton and Noah.

"Hi, Dad," Lawrence said, as he bit into the apple.

"Hi, Lawrence, I'm showin' your friend his quarters." Then he turned back toward Burton. "Welp, dis is it. Home sweet home."

"Hey," Burton said, "I'm not a field hand! I had better quarters in the army." He looked at a straw mattress nestled in a wooden bunk. Dust streamed into the light of the small window over the bed.

"You're not in the army now," Noah said. He walked over to a pitchfork stuck in the straw. He pulled it out and speared it into the bail next to his bunk. After a few seconds, he shifted his yellow straw hat to the back of his head and turned toward Burton. "Dis is the best we can do for ya." Then Noah left the barn.

Burton stood for a while surveying the straw-filled barn. He plucked a piece of straw from the bail and put it in his mouth. It tasted sweet near the back of his tongue. He placed his gun belt on a peg. There was sweat on the inside of the gun belt. He wiped the sweat off on his shirt. Suddenly, he pushed the belt to the back of the peg five times to make absolutely sure it wouldn't fall into the dust. It had to be five times; that was the magic number which made him feel secure. In a rage, he grabbed the pitchfork and threw it at the barn wall. It wedged in just above the stall. "That's what I think of your home sweet home."

"Don't start throwing things around, sarge. Somebody could get hurt," Lawrence said. He pulled the pitchfork out of the wall and threw it back at Burton, it landed at his feet. "I'll see you tomorrow." He turned and started to walk out of the barn, tossing the half-eaten apple into the field through the open door.

"What about the big favor I did for you?" he asked. By now Burton was leaning on one of the stalls and felt the rough chewed up surface from the horses cribbing on the wood.

His question stopped Lawrence from leaving the barn. He turned and faced him, leaning heavily on his good leg. "What favor?" Lawrence asked. "The only favor I remember is me asking you to stop bossing me around."

"You mean saving your life doesn't count? Remember when we were crossing the Mississippi at Vicksburg? I was almost across when I heard you hollering for help, I turned back, grabbed you by the scruff of the neck and pulled you on shore."

"So what's your point?" Lawrence asked.

"You're sleeping in a nice house in your own room with your adopted family—a family that's not even yours. I'm out here in the barn like a farm animal." Burton heard the rustling of Lawrence's bad foot as he approached him with clenched fists dangling by his side.

"I'm sorry you feel that way. We didn't mean for you to be uncomfortable. That's the last thing on my mind."

"Well, it does make me feel like an animal," Burton said. All the while as they talked, Burton had his thumbs hooked in his pants. They were tight against his big belly.

"You're right, sarge. I do owe you a lot. But Abby would feel uncomfortable having you sleeping in the house. I saw what you did at the supper table."

"Come on, kid, I just touched her hand." He sat back down on his bunk leaning up against the barn wall. The wood on the bunk pushed up against the bottom of his legs, making him shift for a more comfortable position.

"We're not in the army anymore, sarge. You can't just do what you want. There are rules out here in civilized society that we have to live by."

"Maybe you have to live by them, not me," Burton said. He lay back on his straw bed with his fingers laced together on the back of his head, looking up at the ceiling of the barn. Then he reached up and fondly tapped his gun that was hanging on the peg. The straw bedding poked him in the back of his head and hands. "How do you know what the war was like?" Burton asked. He got up suddenly, threw his hands in the air, and stared at Lawrence. "You were nothing but a skulker and coffee cooler."

"What do you mean by that?" Lawrence asked. He stood at the ready.

Burton turned his head to the left and spit in the dirt before continuing. "We both know you had a bombproof job a safe distance behind the lines."

"There was no safe distance…not from the big guns. They could reach you anywhere." Burton noticed a far-off look come into Lawrence's eyes. "I can still hear 'em rumbling the ground." Lawrence came over to make peace with Burton. He limped over and put his hand on his left shoulder. "Let's forget about it all right."

Burton twitched as if a hot iron was burning into his shoulder. He grabbed Lawrence's arm and flung it away. "Don't you never touch me again!" he said. "I don't want any of what you got to rub off on me."

"What do you mean? I don't have the pox or anything." Lawrence backed up.

"I mean the disease of cowardice. I can smell it all over you." He leaned forward, sniffed at Lawrence, and chuckled.

"Maybe you're the coward, sarge," he said. "You're stubborn about adapting to civilian life." Then he turned and walked away.

"Turn around"—he reached back and pulled out the gun from his holster and waved it in the air—"I think this adapts me pretty good." Burton felt the confidence well up in his chest while he gripped tightly onto the handle of the gun.

Lawrence turned to face Burton. "You better get some rest. We've got to get up early." Lawrence gave a quick glance at the gun in Burton's hand and then left.

"Who does he think he is, giving me orders?" Burton whispered to himself.

That night, Burton woke up after a restless night of sleep, when the dew was settling on everything, grabbed his blanket and gun and went out to the cornfield behind the barn, crackling through the dry cornstalks in the dark. He swore he saw people moving around in the woods, but he was so tired; that he chose to ignore what he thought he'd seen.

He spread his blanket down in the corner of the fence with his head propped up against it and his pistol resting on his chest. He woke up several times searching for his weapon. His sleep was interrupted with battle dreams. One time, he woke and fired into the woods, thinking that he had seen Johnny Reb and then just as suddenly went back to sleep.

5

FEED THEM

THAT SAME NIGHT, Lawrence went to the summer kitchen and was sitting at the table while a cup of coffee steaming into his face. Abigail sat across from him. He nodded his head, his eyes started to shut.

"You better go to bed," Abigail said. "You're almost swimming in your coffee."

"Okay, Mom." He smiled at her, as he slowly got up and walked toward the stairs. The day still had its dim light scraping at the windows wanting to come in but the night, at eight thirty, was taking over. "You take care of me like a mother hen. I'll see you in the morning." Going up the stairs, he leaned heavily on the railing to support his damaged foot.

"I won't see you till midmorning. I have to go into town," she said, with a full volume in her voice, and then she whispered, "Sleep tight, Lawrence."

He went up to bed, but before he fell asleep, he took another one of his opium pills. He slept a restless sleep.

Even though he was home now with nothing to fear, he still tossed and turned, wrestling with the ghosts of the war.

The morning presented itself with a cacophony of bird chirps at six o'clock in the morning. The sun's yellow light tinted the early dawn horizon. Lawrence got up and made himself ham and eggs. They crackled in the grease of the pan.

The greasy smell reminded him of the stink of gun powder that settled in the valleys after a battle. It should have been the smell of home and safety, but it brought back a fowl stench of death on the battlefield. He leaned his elbows on the table and put his head in his hands, squeezing his temples as hard as he could in order to make the memory of the stink of death go away, and then he breathed into the palms of his hands so that his mind could remember his own breath.

He sat back hard on a chair and let out a deep sigh of relief because the trace of that phantom dissipated into the sweet cloud of roasting coffee. All of a sudden, a man with a leather knapsack rapped on the half-open door, snapping Lawrence back into the newness of the morning.

"Hello, anybody home?" He seemed to be standing at attention.

"What's up, fella?" Lawrence asked, as he got up and marched over to the door.

"I'm hungry." It was a man dressed in a tattered leather vest with a red and white shirt under it. His worn and faded

Union cap covered his long jet-black hair that dropped down over his shoulders. But the most unique thing about him was that he had no right hand, just a nub, and he saluted with it as he stood in the door.

"You don't have to salute me, soldier," Lawrence said.

"Sorry. It's a habit," the soldier said. Lawrence sensed that he thought he had done something horribly wrong because he turned and started to leave.

"Where you going? Come on in." Lawrence pushed open the squeaky door.

He couldn't help noticing that the soldier was surprised about his hospitality, possibly because he had been turned away many times. The soldier at the double turned back around. "Oh thanks, my stomach was a-grumblin' something awful!"

It was the sadness and pleading that came through his eyes that pulled Lawrence toward him. He had seen plenty of severed arms and legs in the war; that's not what impressed him, it was the hopelessness that was reflected in the man's grey eyes. *After all, I'm a maimed soldier too*, he thought.

The pine chair squeaked on the wood floor as Lawrence pulled it out. "Here, sit," he said.

As the man sat down, he reached into his pocket and snapped a three-cent coin on the table. "Is that enough?"

"Put your money away, soldier. I'm not a quartermaster sergeant in the army, this is free."

Lawrence slapped a slab of ham on the plate and slid five fried eggs next to them, and then he poured him a cup of coffee to go along with it. Lawrence smiled as a warm feeling welled up in his chest. The stranger bowed his head and blessed himself with the nub that used to be his hand.

"Where you from, Billy Yank?" Lawrence asked just as he sat down.

"My name is Zack Kearney. I came from around these parts before the War of Rebellion." He took a deep breath as he looked at his plate and then laughed. "Looks good. Army food was so bad it was enough to make a mule desert."

"I remember." Lawrence frowned, imagining the faces of all the starving haggard men.

The breakfast was over and Zack stood up, seeming to snap to attention. But realizing what he was about to do, he stopped and pretended to adjust the straps on his pack. Lawrence smiled at his confusion, knowing that a soldier's training is hard to forget. The hunger had drained from Zack's eyes and satisfaction had replaced it.

"Take some food with you," Lawrence said.

"Gee, thanks, mister." Lawrence opened his backpack and put in biscuits, eggs, bacon, and a bag of coffee.

"There you go, Zack." Lawrence's eyes sparkled with delight, and then he shook the stump of his right hand before he left. He wasn't sure, but he thought he saw tears in the soldier's eyes before he went through the door.

Lawrence watched him awhile through the door as he paused at the edge of the woods. Zack whistled, and five scruffy people emerged from behind the oak trees. A woman with a little girl hugged him, and the others patted him on the back just before they vanished through the curtain of the forest.

After that, Lawrence walked out onto the porch. A procession of wagons and possibly a hundred people trudged up the road. The buckboards and covered wagons rumbled up the hill, while the pots and pans that hung off the back banged against each other. The green and white gingham dresses the women wore were so long that they scrapped along the road, billowing up dust while they walked up the road. The children ran through spaces in the line of people, with skinny dogs yelping and darting after them. One little boy had a mock military uniform on, complete, along with a little sword.

The men, who led the slow-moving mass of people, had their Enfield rifles resting on their shoulders when suddenly the wind began to blow. Some of the men adjusted the bandannas across their faces as they marched up the hill. Others pushed their soft, felt hats securely on their heads. While others took the stiff-looking Union forage caps off and put them in their shirts. And after that, they put their arms in front of their faces to protect themselves from the dust.

In the meantime, Lawrence had hobbled down to the edge of the road. He stood there until the front of the column was near him. "Hey, stop for a second," he shouted. Everyone came to a halt and the noise of the movement up the hill diminished; only coughing, chain rattling from the harnesses, and the playful screams of children could be heard. "I was wondering if you'd like to sit and rest for a while," he said. The frowns and wrinkled brows of the people turned to smiles and laughter.

A man with a black derby on his head slowly walked over to Lawrence after he had handed his rifle to a friend and pulled down his red checkered scarf off his face. "You don't know how welcome that invite is to us," he said. "We've been traveling two days straight."

"Well then, it's time to rest. Pull over here and set up your camp in front of the root cellar. There's plenty of room."

Meanwhile, Burton had come out of the forest and was standing next to the pump, surveying the commotion. He strapped on his gun. "What's up?"—Lawrence quickly hobbled by—"did you hear what I said?"

"Oh, we have visitors. Help me with all the mason jars, will ya?" he asked. He went into the summer kitchen and came out with an armful of glass jars and went over to the people that were getting settled next to the root cellar. He set them down in the grass and went back up to the summer kitchen for more.

Burton sauntered over to the summer kitchen and only picked up two mason jars, one in each hand. He walked leisurely down to where the root cellar was and put them in front of a circle of hungry people. Before they could thank him, he turned and left. On the way up the hill, he spotted Lawrence. "I'm done," Burton said to him at the same time that Lawrence passed by with another armful of canning jars.

"Good, that's good." Lawrence turned his head just as he went down the hill. "Get the stone boat ready. We've got some work to do this morning on the stone wall."

But that's not all that Lawrence had in mind. He went down into the root cellar, where they were storing turnips, cabbages, carrots, potatoes, squash, and onions in baskets along the walls. He found an old brown burlap bag and filled it up with cans of Underwood deviled ham, Borden's condensed milk, Van Camps pork and beans. When he came out, he went over and dumped all the cans on a blanket that was spread out on the lawn. Standing there, he noticed that the ache in his foot had disappeared.

The men pierced the cans with their knives and scooped out every last drop with a spoon. A happy, kind of full feeling tickled Lawrence's chest. He smiled and then chuckled. Then he went back down into the root cellar. "Yeah, this would be great," he said to himself, as he picked up a basket of apples and potatoes, trying to precariously balance the heavy baskets in front of him as he walked up the stairs.

"Here you go," he said, while dumping the delicious red fruit into their laps and then setting down the basket of potatoes. "Take the basket of potatoes with you for later."

"There's a lot of food here," a soldier said, while at the same time he was stabbing at the peaches in the bottom of the glass canning jar and sticking his knife into the red apples.

"Yeah, Noah is a real wizard when it comes to making things sprout up from the dirt," Lawrence said.

Meanwhile, Noah Wilson came up from behind Lawrence. His knees had round wet dirt stains on them. And his overalls were caked with soil. "What's goin' on, Lawrence?" Noah asked. Lawrence was amazed. One minute, when least expected, Noah appeared. Other times, baskets of corn and tomatoes were piled up at the end of the field, almost as if he had imaginary elves helping him through the day.

But Lawrence realized that Daniel was the magical elf that he was thinking about. Last night, Lawrence peaked into his room and didn't find him there. In the early morning, when he got up and looked out the window, he saw baskets of corn, yellow squash, and green cucumbers sitting in baskets at the end of the rows of plants waiting impatiently to be picked up.

"Just feeding some hungry people," Lawrence said. Lawrence waited for some reaction from Noah. He wondered whether he had overstepped his authority by giving these people the stored food that was supposed to be for the wintertime.

Noah, with his thumbs hooked into the top of his overalls, stood silent for a minute and surveyed the soldiers and their families. "It's okay, son. Dis is sorta like that mince pie ya couldn't let go ta waste, huh? Any way, we owe these soldiers a lot more than just food," he said, and then with the sound of rustling leaves and the parting of corn stalks, he disappeared into the field of corn next to the house.

A hundred people gathered under the old elm tree. They all sat in a circle. In the middle of the circle was Lawrence. He was handing out slices of mince and peach pie. And everywhere on the lawn there were opened tin cans and canning jars.

Most of the men had large black hobnailed boots on while others had leather-soled, high-topped shoes. Many of the men had suspenders on over their striped shirts. It was a motley group of vagabond men along with their ragtag wives and children standing close to them. The only thing they had in common was their hunger.

Abigail came up the hill in the buckboard after going to town. When she drove up, every man tipped his hat, from broad-brimmed slouch hats to natty bowlers to derbies. Almost every soldier had a hat on, and the ones that didn't bowed their heads in respect.

Lawrence pointed with a nod of his head toward Abigail. "That's the lady that was gracious enough to let you have all this food," Lawrence said.

"Thanks, ma'am!" They all said simultaneously. The chorus of the voices of the families echoed through the trees.

"Lawrence!" she shouted. "Can I talk to you for a minute?" He walked through the men, like Moses parting the Red Sea and went up to the buckboard.

"Those are the fruits and vegetables I canned for the winter. What are we suppose to do now?"

"Abby, I'm surprised at you. Where's your humanity? Look at those people."

She turned and looked at them milling about under the tree. Some of the men took off their worn-out shoes and massaged their bare feet, and some pulled up their worn-out trousers. A young woman opened up bedrolls and knapsacks that were so tattered as to be unrecognizable. The women's dresses were patched and when the children ran by, their scraps of clothes flapped like thin flags on their skinny bodies. Not much talk went through the crowd, just the sound of rattling and clanking of the metal cups and plates.

"I see what you mean," she said. "I should have understood." Turning back slowly to Lawrence, her eyes filled with tears.

"Abby, you don't know what it is to be hungry. To have to eat hardtack soaked in coffee for a week."

"No, I guess I don't," she said.

6

THE HABIT OF KILLING

AFTER ALL THE people were fed, Lawrence walked back up to the barn. Burton stood next to the stoneboat waiting for instructions. The Morgan horse that was hitched to the stoneboat was known affectionately as Rebel. Lawrence got on the flat wooden platform and wrapped his arms around the reins to steady the horse. The horse swished flies away with its tail and stamped its hoof into the ground.

"Da wall has to be fixed an' I only have a week to do it," Noah said. He started to walk away when suddenly he spun back around. "Oh, almost forgot. There's a ditch with gravel in it. Fill it in."

Then Lawrence slapped Rebel on the rump with the reins, making the stoneboat lurch forward. The metal wedges and hand tools chimed as the car buffeted and slithered from side to side. Lawrence steered the horse to the soft side of the road. The bow of the boat sliced through the dirt, parting it like a wave on a lake. He was hypnotized by the parting wave and imagined himself on the water while Burton sat in the back. The high-pitched whine of locust and the "caw" of the crows welcomed the two veterans to the abundant cornfield.

Another fantasy invaded his mind while riding the wooden stoneboat. He imagined himself riding in a chariot like Achilles going into battle with the Trojans. But all those musings came to a sudden halt when he was jolted out of his daydream by the sound of shots behind him.

Burton was shooting at a flock of crows at the edge of the cornfield. He rested the colt pistol over his left arm. The shots kicked up the dust in the middle of the flock of crows, making them scatter into the air.

"What the hell are you doing?" Lawrence looked over his shoulder while steadying the horse.

"Look at those crows fly, just like Johnny Rebs." Burton continued to cock the pistol and shoot at the birds in the air until his gun was empty.

Lawrence finally pulled the boat to a standstill. He got off and wrapped the reins around a large rock. By this time, Burton turned around and was facing him.

"Don't you think we've seen enough killing?" Lawrence said. He rested his left arm on the horse's flank. "I know I sure have."

Burton dropped his .44-caliber Colt revolver back into the holster. Lawrence jumped at Burton and tried to grab the gun, but Burton was too strong. The men wrestled and fell onto the stoneboat. While this was happening, the horse stared back at the struggling men. In an instant, the horse bolted down the dusty road toward the stone wall. They turned into a cornfield and plowed down the whole row from the road to the edge of the forest.

Meanwhile, Burton grabbed the five-foot crowbar and was pushing it against Lawrence's throat. Lawrence tossed it off into the dirt. When the horse turned back onto the road, the stoneboat flipped over and dumped the men out. Rebel, the horse, continued into the woods and finally got the boat snagged in some wild grapevines near the stone wall.

Lawrence managed to pull Burton's gun out of his holster and throw it into the field. Almost without hesitation, the sergeant ran after his gun. It landed on an overripe tomato. He picked it up and wiped it off on his shirt. Enraged, he picked up a rock and ran back toward Lawrence.

Just in time, the young soldier saw him throw the rock. He ducked to one side as it passed by his head and he heard it whoosh by his ear. At that moment, Abigail rode up in the wagon and interrupted the fight. Both men stared not knowing what to do. Then Burton, without warning, ran into the woods.

"Lawrence, what's going on?" she asked. She scooted over on the seat and leaned down so that she could be closer to Lawrence.

"I'll tell you in a second." He went into the woods and unharnessed Rebel from the stoneboat and tied him to the back of the buckboard.

"Move! We've got to get the law." Lawrence jumped onto the seat, pushing Abby over as he grabbed the reins from her hands. Then he turned the horse hard back to the barn. He whipped the reins over its rump so Abby had to hold onto her bonnet to keep it from flying off.

"Can you tell me what this is all about?" she shouted over the clatter of the wagon.

Lawrence hollered back. "He tried to kill me." He pulled back hard on the reins when he finally got to the barn. The horse came to a skidding halt. "I'll meet you back at the barn this afternoon but for now stay in the house. Unhitch Rebel and put him in a stall." After she put the horse in the barn, he drove off to tell his story to the sheriff in town. On the way, he took yet another opium pill because his foot hurt after the fight.

At noon, they met in the barn. Lawrence came hobbling in just as a downpour caught him at the door. He took off his cap and slapped it on his leg to get it dry. "If this keeps up, we'll never finish that wall. Hi, Abby."

"It's over now, isn't it?" Abby asked. Her eyes pleaded for an answer.

"I think so. Me and the sheriff looked for him in the woods but couldn't find him."

The excitement of the moment and the innocent and vulnerable expression on her face made Lawrence go over and sit on the bale of hay next to her. He pulled her close to him and kissed her on the lips; she didn't pull away but settled in his arms. After a while, he embraced her tenderly. But as time went on, he became passionate, and the memories of being like brother and sister faded away.

He held her tighter every time a clap of thunder shook the barn. *It's like holding onto a young frightened lamb*, he thought. And that feeling only made him want her more. Suddenly, she went limp. Lawrence looked at her in surprise. She was staring at the open door with a look of terror. Burton stood with his pistol pointing at them, and every time the lightning flashed, it silhouetted his rain-soaked figure.

"Well, well, how quaint. The two lovers in a loving embrace," he said. "Move aside!" He waved the gun at Abby. His rain-soaked clothes dripped onto the floor of the barn. "My business is with him." Lawrence stood up anticipating the impact of the bullet.

"I don't know what you think I've done," he said, raising his hands into the air.

"It's not what you've done, but what you didn't do. I see the faces of the boys I sent to their deaths in my dreams every night. But your face isn't one of them, and it should be."

Abby moved to a pillar nearby and wrapped her arms around it so her shaking knees wouldn't collapse under her. A clap of thunder shook the building. "Burton," she said as if speaking to a child. "The war is over, and the Greeks sailed back home."

His forehead furrowed and his eyes squinted. He didn't understand a word she said, but it was just enough distraction for Lawrence to pounce on the unsuspecting sergeant. They rolled on the barn floor with the heavy pistol held high above their heads.

"Stay there, Abby," Lawrence shouted the order just as he got control of the gun and got up with it in his hand.

She started to run out the door but abruptly turned back into the barn. "No, I can't leave," she whispered to herself. Lawrence heard her. Then she ran back to his side. He held her close.

Lawrence stood there with the gun in his hand, waving it around as he made his points. The situation was different now and Burton realized it. The sick expression on his face told Lawrence he was expecting a bullet in his gut any moment. "Listen, sir, maybe you're right, maybe we haven't treated you with respect," Lawrence said. "Maybe it's time to change all that. What do you think about that idea?"

A dumbfounded expression came over Burton's face. And every muscle on his body relaxed. "Now you're talking"—he walked with care to a bale of hay and sat down—"but you don't have to call me sir. I'm just a sergeant, you know."

"It's just a sign of respect, sarge," Lawrence said. Then he walked over to Burton and handed him his gun.

"Thanks." He looked down at his gun resting in his lap and then at Lawrence. His eyes opened wide. He slipped the pistol into its holster after the shock of getting his gun back had worn off.

"You're welcome."

"What are you doing, Lawrence? He'll kill us all." Abby pulled him aside and whispered in his ear.

"No, Abigail, we have to work together from now on," he said. "Here's what's happening. We both brought back a sickness from the war, a sickness in our minds, a trotting heart, and a rage against life. Besides, I need his help on the farm. I can't do it all with this bum leg I've got." Then he turned to Burton. "Tell me what I can do to fix the gap that's come between us?"

Burton stood up and hooked his thumbs on his gun belt. "Well, for one thing, I want to move into the house. And I want some new clothes and a hot bath."

"You got it," Lawrence said. "Don't forget your bag."

"There's no way I'm forgetting this bag. I think we should divide up the loot right now."

"What do you mean?" Lawrence walked over to Burton while he was opening the white burlap bag and pulling out gold ingots and bags of gold coins.

"This is your share," Burton said. On top of a bale of hay were five small rectangular blocks of gold along with a bag of coins. "You mean you forgot about all the stuff we took from Johnny Reb. Some of this is yours."

"I don't want it," Lawrence said. "That's the stuff we got from the rebs that were in the stockade, right?"

"That's right," Burton said. "What's the matter, don't you want any?"

"No, there's blood on it"—he walked over and picked up one of the small ingots and scraped his fingernail over it—"these are nothing but lead painted with gold paint."

Burton stared at Lawrence and shook his head. "Let me see that," he said. He snatched it out of Lawrence's hand. "I've been had." He picked up the other gold and scraped it with the barrel tip of his gun. "You know, you're right. They're nothing but lead."

"How about the jewelry you got in that bag? Do you think that's real or fake?" Abigail asked.

"Take a look at it, Miss Abby," Burton demanded.

First, she looked at Lawrence to get his approval. He nodded, indicating that she should go and see what she could find out. She picked up the jewelry in her hand. It hung between her fingers. "They look like glass. I'm sorry, but I don't think they're real." Then she dropped them back into the bag and walked over to Lawrence, nestling into his side while they both looked at Burton.

"Those dam rebs. They cheated me!" He fired his gun into the bag and also at the fake gold bars.

"You feel better now?" Lawrence asked.

"Yeah, a little bit," Burton said.

"Get Rebel and we'll go back out to the stone wall," Lawrence said.

They all stood in the open door of the barn, staring out at the rain as it came down in sheets. "I'm going into the house," Abigail said, at the same time, she ran out the door, through the rain and into the summer kitchen.

"This is impossible. We'll have to wait to see if it stops. I don't know what we're going to do. The wall has to be built," Lawrence said. The storm was a New England nor'easter sending torrents of rain and wind against the fields of corn, flattening them against the ground. And swelling the calm streams into angry, fast-moving rivers.

7

PROTECTION

BURTON RAN TO the house with his bedroll tucked under his arm. Lawrence scooted back to the house the best way he could, and at last, they all met in the summer kitchen. They stamped their feet on the wooden floor and pulled at their pants and shirts to flip off the rain. Puddles of rain collected on the floor.

"Look what you've done," Abigail said as she swept the puddles out the door. "Stay right there. I'll be right back," she ordered. A minute later, she returned with a handful of towels. "Here, use these." She flipped open some of the towels and put them on the floor; the others she handed to the two soldiers.

"Thanks," Lawrence said. He tried to dry off every inch of his body by pressing the towels down hard on his shirt and his pants. He even tried to dry his hobnailed boots. He handed the soaking wet towels back to Abigail. She threw the towels into the sink.

But Burton ignored her and took off his shirt and squeezed it dry over the sink. Then he slapped it against the icebox and slung it over his shoulder. It still dripped on the floor.

Burton left the room and went into the sitting room while Abigail and Lawrence stayed in the summer kitchen. Lawrence sighed and sat down hard on the seat. The rains clattered on the roof, and the thunder echoed over the cornfields. Abigail focused her eyes on Lawrence.

Something quickened in Abigail's heart when she looked at Lawrence. "I think you're still handsome," she said. "You ripened into a man. I really didn't recognize you at first. But I still can't help seeing the boy inside the man."

Lawrence's eyes smiled at her. "Abby, get me a mirror," he asked.

She ran out of the room and came back with a handheld mirror. "Here." She handed it to him and stood back to see what he was going to do.

He looked into the mirror and talked to the image and said, "Yes, Lawrence, you are really handsome. You sort of look like Achilles."

"Oh stop, Lawrence." She took the mirror away, and then she gave him a playful poke in the ribs.

Her tenderness oozed from every pore as she stood over Lawrence. A warmth and understanding glowed from her face. It was as if she had reached into her chest and took out her heart and placed it in front of him saying, "See, this is me."

A pleading expression came over her face as if she was expecting him to respond to her in the same way, but when he didn't, she folded her arms in front of her. She was in a snit. Suddenly, she threw her neckerchief at Lawrence, excused herself, and strode close in front of him.

"Ha ha," he snickered. When she went by, he reached out and grabbed her, stopping her forward motion, then sitting her on his lap. She leaned forward and laughed a little bit and then kissed him on the lips. She put her index finger over Lawrence's mouth.

"Don't say a word," she demanded. "I just want to sit here together."

"Okay," he said softly. She rested her head on his shoulder.

Piercing through their loving silence and embrace came the guttural clearing of Burton's throat from the other room.

"I guess we've got to show Burton his new room," Lawrence whispered in Abigail's little ear.

"All right," she said. She showed her disgust by shaking her head from side to side and then saying, "Ach. I guess we have to."

With that, they both got up and went into the sitting room. Burton was rocking in a delicate rocking chair; the chair creaked under the strain. Abigail cringed as she watched the drops of rain drop off his hair and from his wet shirt onto the rug. He was out of place among the lace curtains in the window, the exotic palm and flower plants in large pots next to the curtains, and the pink frilly edged pillows on the sofa.

"Come on, sarge, we'll show you where you're going to bunk," Lawrence said.

They all walked by the fireplace, but Lawrence all at once stopped and grabbed the poker that was leaning up against the cast-iron kettle, all black and gray and soot covered, it hung off to the side.

He poked at the logs supported by the squat claw-foot andiron. They were being consumed by the yellow fire, making them spit out sparks into the living room. "Boy, we could have used the heat from this fire during winter quarters in sixty-three and sixty-four. The battery was parked, the horses were turned over to the horse sergeant, and the guns were stowed away. It was the chilling rain, the cutting sleet, and the drifting snow that I remember the most." It surprised Abigail that even Burton looked into the fire with nostalgia.

She could appreciate what the two men had gone through from Lawrence's description. She understood their contentment at being at ease and enjoying the respite in winter quarters. There was no more marching, no more shooting, no more killing.

"Yeah, it was cold and with a lot of snow. But at least in winter quarters, we could eat our fill and lick our wounds,"

Burton said. She saw him come out of his trance after being hypnotized by the fire and say, "Well, show me where I'm going to sleep." The animosity she felt for Burton seemed to fade away as she noticed him looking into the fire.

After that, they all walked upstairs. The stairs were painted a light cream color and each riser had painted images of oak leaves, elm leaves, and fern leaves on them, and at the very top riser was a picture of the farmhouse.

They entered the room which had a marble top mirrored dresser and a laborer's rope bed and a small washstand in it. Burton slid the feather mattress on to the bed and then tossed his bedroll on top of it, holding the pistol in his hand; he plopped down on the bed. The gun rested on his chest.

He looked around the room. "Home sweet home. This is a might better than the barn, I'd say. Yeah, this will do just fine."

Maybe now things will get back to normal, Abigail thought.

They walked out of the room. Abigail shut the door behind them, and they stood in the hallway for a while standing close to each other, even as they talked.

"Burton and you always seem worried and angry. Is it just my imagination?" she asked as she grabbed hold of both of his arms. He did a slight shrug of his shoulders and cleared his throat.

"No, it isn't. Like I said before, you have to be patient with us. We're damaged goods."

"Even when we're near each other, I feel like your body is close but your mind is far away." She leaned into Lawrence, put her arms around his waist and rested her head on his chest. His heart was beating hard and fast in her ear.

"Let's go down to the sitting room and talk," Lawrence suggested with a little smile on his face.

"That's another thing," Abigail said. "We seem to never be alone so we can talk. Burton is skulking around or my dad is close by. And I feel like I'm in a war zone all the time. There's no Johnny Rebs here."

"I know, I know," he said, walking down the stairs in front of her like all gentlemen did at that time. Lawrence talked with his head down. She descended the stairs behind him. The clock in the sitting room struck at three o'clock.

A minute later, they rocked in two spindle-backed rocking chairs next to the window and under her uncle Jeremiah's picture. The fire crackled and then popped. Lawrence jumped, almost falling off the chair.

"Are you all right?" Abigail asked. All of a sudden, she reached out and steadied the rocking chair. "That's what I mean. What are you afraid of?"

"It's deeper than that. It's not just fear. It's a numbness and anger that I can't get rid of. What I really am afraid of is losing you. What if I can't stop what's going on inside my head?" He pushed back, rocking the chair away from Abigail.

"No," she said. "You'll never lose me." She rocked back toward Lawrence.

Lawrence smiled at her. "I've got a present that I think you'll like."

"A present? That's so unexpected, Lawrence. I would've never guessed," she said with a twinkle in her eye.

He got up. "Hold on! Stay right here," he said. She saw him leave the room and go through the summer kitchen and toward the barn. She rocked back and forth smiling to herself and looking up to the ceiling wistfully. She had visions of them being married and living happily ever after. But it seemed as if he was taking a hundred years to get back to the sitting room.

"I wish he'd get back. I can't stand it," she said to herself. Then she pushed hard on the rocking chair in frustration, bumping it against the wall. At that instant, Lawrence came limping through the kitchen and into the sitting room.

The storm was still raging, the rain coming down in sheets, the lightning streaking across the sky, the thunder rumbling over the house. Lawrence dripped a path of water from the kitchen into the sitting room.

He had a hollow, six-foot long round piece of wood that he held next to his hip, with five yellow ribbons tied to it and a white ribbon on one end. "This is a courting stick, Abby. It's so we can talk to each other and nobody will be able to hear what were saying"—he placed the stick in front of her, it stretched halfway across the room—"now we won't have any problem."

"How does it work?" she asked.

"I talk in one end of the hollow stick, and you put it to your ear. And when you want to talk to me, I put it to my ear."

"I love it," she said. "Let's talk to each other." They picked up the long stick, taking turns talking into it and then listening. Abigail giggled and Lawrence laughed.

After a while, Lawrence took his turn. "Abby, put the stick to your ear," he said. "Can you hear me?" She nodded yes. "Hey, missy, take the white ribbon that's tied onto your side of the stick and open up the silk bag that it's attached to."

She untied the ribbon and pulled open the strings on the white satin bag. She dumped the contents into the palm of her hand. It was a large rose-cut diamond ring surrounded by many small rose cuts set in silver on gold. "Oh my god, Lawrence!" She stared at the ring in disbelief. "What does this mean? Is it what I think it means?" she asked. Her heart pounded, and she could barely catch her breath.

"Yes, my darling. Will you marry me?" He kneeled in front of her and took her hands and kissed them. "I'd be the luckiest man in the world if you said yes."

"Of course, I'll marry you, Lawrence Ellsworth," she said. Her cheeks flushed and her skin tingled.

"That's what I've wanted to hear ever since I came back from the war." Then he stood up, pulling her up with him so they stood together in an embrace. He whispered in her ear. "I love you, Abigail Wilson."

"No, I'm Abigail Ellsworth now," she said, glancing at the ring on her finger.

"That was my grandmother's ring and then my mothers," he said. "Do you like it?"

"Oh yes. It's the most beautiful thing that I ever saw." Then they kissed.

All of a sudden, a shot cracked open the silence, and Burton stood at the top of the stairs waving his gun around above his head. The bullet split the courting stick in half. "I see two copperheads down there," he shouted and then pointed the gun at the couple.

"Go in the kitchen, Abby, quick," Lawrence said as he pushed her in that direction.

"You stay right where you are," Burton said while pointing the gun at Abigail.

Abigail froze and with wide eyes watched in horror while Burton descended the set of steps with a glazed look on his face. When he got to the bottom of the stairs, the gun was still trained on her.

Lawrence saw his opportunity and grabbed the poker out of the fireplace and slashed at his hand, making him drop the pistol. But Burton would not be delayed in the killing of his imaginary enemy. He grabbed the poker out of Lawrence's hand and pinned him against one of the rockers, pushing it against his neck. Lawrence coughed and struggled to push the sergeant away.

Abigail picked up the gun—a heavy gun—so heavy that she had a hard time holding it level and straight. She held it in both hands knowing full well what she had to do, and it made her sad and sick inside but determined. She cocked the gun and fired. The smoke from the gun hung in the air. The room became silent except for the crackle of the logs in the fireplace. Then the sound of a metallic thump of the gun on the rug broke the silence as Abigail dropped it, preoccupied with what she had just done.

Lawrence pushed the lifeless hulk of a man off him and onto the rug. He stared at Abigail. She stood still except for her shoulders. They shook as she sobbed and hung her head.

"What else could I do? He was going to kill you," she said soon after she stopped crying.

"Yes, you're right," he said and at the same time got up, put his arm around her waist and escorted her into the summer kitchen. They sat there; Abigail, with her elbows on the table and her hands folded in front of her mouth, glancing into the sitting room at the mound of flesh that used to be Burton. Lawrence stood in back of her, resting his hands on her shoulders.

"I was so happy when you gave me your ring," she said. "Then this had to happen."

"I think it was inevitable, Abby."

"Yes," she said. Her eyes glazed over and she became numb, and her body disconnected from her mind. "Yes… Yes," she kept saying while staring into the nothingness of space.

"Snap out of it, Abby. We've got to do something about the body," Lawrence said. He walked around to face her.

Abigail little by little looked up at Lawrence as if he were a ghost. "What, oh the body. Yes, the body," she said.

"I have an idea. I'm going to get the buckboard. Will you be all right if I leave you alone?" He left in a hurry.

"Alone…Yes, I'll be okay," she said, talking to the blank walls and an empty kitchen.

In the corner behind the pantry door came the shuffling of feet on the wood floor. "Lawrence…Pa, is that you?" she asked. "Hello."

"No, Miss Abigail, it's me Daniel," he said. His hands and knees were shaking as he came into the kitchen.

"How long have you been out there, Daniel?"

"Long time, ma'am."

"How long?"

"Long enough," he said.

"Then you saw what happened?"

"Yes, I saw it all and was scared to come out."

"You don't have to be afraid of me or Lawrence or Pa. The one that you should have been afraid of is dead." Daniel's appearance snapped her out of her daze, so she became as sober as a judge. Her survival instinct was taking over, and her mind became crystal clear and deliberate.

"I owe you people a lot. You took me in as an equal farmhand when nobody else would touch me. What can I do to help you, Miss Abigail?" He asked her, clasping his hands in front of him and standing perfectly still, waiting for her orders.

She looked Daniel deep in his brown eyes and asked, "What did you see?"

"Well, I seen…Oh, I understand, Miss Abigail," he said. "I ain't seen nothin'. I wasn't even here." Thinking that, after all, he had nothing to lose by keeping quiet, he winked at Abigail, and then left through the back door of the house and went into the fields.

8

AN EVIL IS BURIED

MEANWHILE, LAWRENCE HAD driven the buckboard to the back of the house, tied Rebel to the porch, and walked back into the summer kitchen. He became jittery, and he was unable to make a decision about what to do about Burton. A dark silence followed him into the kitchen as he looked down at Abigail. They both stared into each other's eyes searching for a glimmer of a solution, and then at the same time, turned and stared at the heap of flesh and bones in the living room that used to be a man.

Abigail had gotten a cotton quilt from the closet and had draped it across her shoulders. It was red, white, and blue. Its white background had red stars on it with an eight-star flag in the middle. She held it close to her cheeks with both hands.

"I know what we'll do"—Lawrence walked over to the living room and stared at Burton—"we'll bury him. We'll bury him under the wall."

"I'm scared, Lawrence," Abigail said. She dropped the quilt down to her shoulders. "We shouldn't be doing this."

Without looking back at Abigail, Lawrence went into the sitting room and picked Burton up under his shoulders. The touch of his body was cold and leathery as he dragged him along. While pulling him, the sound of his hobnail boots scraped along the rug and then sounded louder over the hardwood floor. He struggled with the heavy body. Abigail got up and helped him. They each took an arm and pulled him out the door, on to the porch, and down the steps of the entrance to the kitchen. His heavy boots clunked, clunked, clunked down the steps until he lay on the ground on the back of the buckboard in a heap. The weather had calmed down, and a misty drizzle filled the air.

"Help me put him in the back of the wagon," Lawrence asked. He was already grunting while he lifted and pushed the lifeless hulk up halfway into the buckboard. He tossed the pistol in along with the body. It made a sickening thud on the wooden floor of the carriage.

"Okay," she said. She moved little by little toward the body, uncertain and reluctant to touch the dead corpse. But finally, she helped lift and shove the body into the back of the carriage. All at once, she backed away and put her hands to her mouth as she stared at Burton. Then she ran into the summer kitchen and got the quilt. She came out and threw the comforter over the lifeless body. "I couldn't stand looking at him," she said.

Lawrence noticed her reaction to the body and became aware of her fear. To him, it was a natural occurrence every day in the war. It was accepted that people were going to die. But here and now, he expected that kind of thing to end. He had a hope that that evil had been left behind, and as he looked at Burton lying there, he knew that a part of that iniquity would be buried along with him. For that he was glad, but for bringing this malevolence to the farm that he loved so much, he felt guilty. He got into the spring seat of the buckboard and shook his head, feeling that somehow he was responsible for all that was going wrong.

"Are you all right?" Lawrence asked Abigail, looking down at her. "You don't have to come."

"I want to help you. You shouldn't have to do this alone," she said. Then she got into the squeaky seat next to him and patted his hand. "You can't leave me behind. It makes the thing easier when it's spread out between the two of us. Besides, I'm the one that shot him."

"I know." After that, he whipped the reins over the back side of Rebel, and they were off down the path that led through the field and into the woods. Lawrence could hear the bump, bump of the body and the clang of the shovel in the bed of the carriage. Under the seat was a bottle of whiskey that rolled around, thudding against the wooden sides of the carriage.

They went through the fields, past the tall green corn plants, next to the bushy tomatoes and on to the road that led to the end of the fields and the beginning of the newly constructed stone walls.

They paused at the wall. A ditch was built for the fence three feet deep and five feet wide. This is where Lawrence was going to put the body.

He knew from watching them build the stone fences as a boy that they only put the heaviest rocks in the bottom of the ditch. The base had wide stones, and after that, the smaller stones on top like the construction of the ancient pyramids.

He thought, *How meticulous the stone masons were as they read the contours of each rock.* All the stones had a story to tell to the experienced eye of the mason. Some were too round, some too flat, only the rocks with just the right surface were picked. They wanted the wall to stand for a thousand years. A millennium would be just about right to hide Burton's body. The gravity of all those stones pushing down on the wall would keep it where it was put.

Lawrence pulled the blanket off the body and wrapped it around Abigail. "Here, keep this around you. You look cold," he said. She shivered from the shock of the experience. "Here, take a swig of this." He reached under the seat and came up with a bottle of whiskey. He popped the cork, and she took a long, deep swig of the alcohol. Lawrence got off the seat and stood next to her, rubbing her arm to comfort her and at the same time gazing at the body.

She coughed and then tried to catch her breath. "What was that stuff?" she asked.

"It's what we used to call 'Bust-Head' whiskey," he said. "I made it myself. Do you like it?"

"Sort of. We need something for courage. It might as well be something you made."

He took the bottle away from her and gulped half of it down. "Yeah, that's what I think too. That's why I brought it along."

"I want some more," she said as she reached down and took the bottle out of Lawrence's hand.

"Take it easy, Abby. That's pretty powerful stuff." He reached over to her and pulled the bottle out of her mouth. The alcohol spilled all over her dress. "You're done."

"We have to tell da law about dis, don't we?" Abigail asked. The powerful homemade whiskey was taking effect. She sniffled, her teeth chattered, and she swayed back and forth when she talked.

"I don't know, maybe we shouldn't say anything to anybody!"

"What are you sayin'? I just killed somebody." She turned her face to Lawrence and blinked her eyes, trying to focus on his image.

"No, it was both of us," he said. Then he bent down and picked up the pistol from the bed of the carriage. He pulled back the trigger and fired into the lifeless corpse. Abigail jumped. "Now we're both guilty."

All of a sudden, Lawrence went to the back of the buckboard and dragged the body off and onto the ground. A moldy damp smell came from the ground, as he bent over the body, and that's when he became conscious that the pain in his foot was gone. He got on his knees and pushed the heavy ebony bulk into the ditch. He heard a splash and then a thump. To put a fitting end to the sergeant's life, Lawrence felt that it was appropriate to toss the gun into the grave too. Finally, it was done.

He got the shovel and started to scoop gravel and then dirt into the hole. When he was satisfied that there was enough dirt in the hole, he went over to a large flat rock and slid it down the wet slippery side of the ditch, until it rested on top of the dirt. He did this twice more until there were three large flat rocks on top of the grave. After that, he plopped back on the tail of the buckboard, glad that the incident was all over.

9

THE WHOLE TRUTH

BY NOW, LAWRENCE and Abigail were pulling up to the back of the house. It was still early afternoon. As it happened, when they turned the corner, they met up with Noah Wilson and Daniel. Abigail lay down in the back of the buckboard passed out from the whiskey.

"What's wrong with Abigail," Noah asked. He took long strides over to the wagon. His heart dropped when he saw her all spread out in the back of the wagon. "Is she still alive?" he asked, while reaching down, smoothing back her hair and patting her on the cheek, trying to wake her up.

"She's okay, Pa," Lawrence said, turning toward Noah. "She just had a little bit too much to drink."

"Oh. She don't drink," he said. "I'm bringin' her in the house."

"Okay."

Noah picked Abigail up like a new born calf in his arms. The sadness and concern for her ate at his insides. He gazed at her as he carried her into the house. He thought back when she was a baby and how she needed him around all the time, at the same time as he carried her through the kitchen and upstairs into her room. It took as much energy to care for her as it did to care for the farm. Now, she was an important part of the workings of the farm and had to be able to do her chores. He placed her on the bed and put a pillow under her head before he left the room.

When he passed the next room, he noticed a white canvass bag and a bedroll still at the foot of the bed.

Noah defined himself by his experiences as a farmer. He had a deep investment in this life, just as his father before him. He loved his daughter, but everything in the farm had to pull its weight; she was no exception.

He walked back down stairs and into the kitchen where Lawrence and Daniel were already sitting at the kitchen table.

"Daniel, make some caw-fee, will ya?" Noah asked. Daniel went to the counter and started to make the coffee. The clang of the pot and the cups echoed through the air. In a frenzy, he pulled out the chair straight across from Lawrence, sat hard on the seat, and at once began laying down the law to him.

"I can see you're upset, Pa," Lawrence said. "What's wrong?"

The rage that he felt after seeing Abigail drunk seethed in his gut, but like everything else, he controlled it. "Do ya think that there's anythin' that goes on in dis farm that I dunno about?" Noah asked. At that instant, Daniel cautiously placed the porcelain blue and white cups of coffee on the table and backed away, not wanting to be in the middle of the battle.

"No. I suppose you know everything," Lawrence said, and then he picked up his cup of coffee and took a sip.

"I know Abby's not like your sister anymore. Do you think I'm blind," he asked.

"No."

"Treat her like your future wife, not like a buddy. Protect her," he said.

"Okay, Pa, I understand."

Just as Noah took a swallow of coffee, Abigail appeared at the entrance to the kitchen.

"Hello, Miss Abby," Daniel said.

She staggered into the room and immediately sat at the table and put her head down on the surface. "Oh my head," she said. "It feels like a sack of potatoes."

"Oh, where's Burton?" Noah asked. "Haven't seen him all mornin'. Were those bags I saw in da room upstairs his?

A silence filled the room like a heavy fog and nobody said a word, until Lawrence broke the silence. "He…ah… left, yeah that's it. He just quit and went away," he said.

"Why you lyin' to me? I saw his bags still in his room," Noah said. He took a swig and then stared at Lawrence over the steaming coffee. The little ceramic cup looked like a toy in his muscular hand.

"You'll find out eventually anyway," Lawrence said. "I, ah…I…ah…shot him with his own pistol. It was an accident. He would have killed me if I didn't defend myself."

Daniel was standing next to the wall, and as soon as he heard that, he slid down to his rump. Then he said to himself, "Mercy me. We got trouble now."

Noah, with a scowl on his face, leered over at him as he was slumped down in a ball in the corner of the kitchen. "Daniel, go outside. Dis is none of your affair."

"No, Pa. He already knows," Abigail said. She slowly picked up her head and turned to face her father.

"He knows?"

"Yes, he was there all the time. He saw the whole thing," she said as she dropped her head back down on the table with a clunk and covered it with her arms. Her voice was muffled because she talked into the top of the table. "And since we're telling the truth, it wasn't Lawrence that shot him, it was me. We buried him under the wall in the north pasture."

"I guess I dunno everything that goes on in the farm after all," Noah said.

He stared into his coffee.

With that, Abigail got up and sat on Lawrence's lap. "We love each other," Abigail said.

Noah looked up at the couple. "Yeah I know," he said. "Since we're tellin' the truth, I might as well be honest with you, Abby."

"What is it, Pa?"

"I'm not your pa and you're not my daughter. You're adopted, just like Lawrence." Noah could see the shock on everybody's face while looking around the room. In point of fact, his purpose in blurting out that hidden truth was to make Abigail look at reality. Everything in his world was concrete. Everybody came after the farm in importance; even he was a slave to the established routine.

"But I remember seeing my mother's face staring down at me when I was a baby," she said.

"Dat wasn't your real mother. It was my wife, Miranda. Do you remember when you were ten and she died from cholera?"

"Yes, I do, but that doesn't matter," Abigail said. "You're the only father, and she's the only mother I've ever known."

Noah got up from the table and went over to the window. He stood there a long time looking at the farm and the fields beyond. Everybody in that little room was affected by what was said. But out of all those people, he seemed most moved, most changed.

He turned back around and faced everybody in the kitchen. "The farm has to be saved. Without you, children, there is no farm. There is no future," Noah said. "Come on, Lawrence, Daniel, follow me."

"Where are we going?" Lawrence asked.

"We're goin' ta finish that wall in the north pasture," Noah said.

"What about me, Pa?" Abigail asked. "Can I come along too?"

"Okay," he said. "Jus stay out ov' the way. We got a lot of work to do."

They all got in the buckboard and went to the wall. Noah and Abigail rode on the seat while Lawrence and Daniel sat in the back. The shovels, the hammers, the crowbar, and the chisels bounced every time the wagon hit a bump in the road.

⸺⸺◈⸺⸺

When they stopped, Abigail got off the seat and went into the forest. "I'm going to go and pick some blueberries, Pa," she said as she disappeared into the woods.

"Okay, don't go too far. We might need ya," he said.

A flattened out road of dirt ran the length of the unfinished wall.

"Where is he?" Noah asked.

"Over there," Lawrence pointed to the end of the pile of rocks.

Noah went over and packed down the three flat rocks with his foot. "Dis is where we'll put the end of the wall." He put on his gloves and moved the rocks around; they would become the footing for the wall. Then he got little pieces of stone and wedged them between the large rocks.

The next thing he did was a ritual that he performed every time he built anything on the farm. He went into the field of corn next to the wall and came out with a yellow stalk of corn. He reached into his pocket and shaved off a few kernels with his knife and placed them on a corner stone that was to be used to finish off the end of the wall. Then he poured some of the whiskey over the corn and undid the little screw cap from the Hurricane lantern. He dumped oil over the corn and whiskey.

"Pa, why do you do that," Lawrence asked, looking up from his position seated on a large boulder.

"Oh…it's somethin' my dad taught me a long time ago. His teacher, a Scottish mason, Angus McBride, told my dad it was for good luck."

"Does it work?"

"Seems to," Noah said.

Meanwhile, Daniel and Lawrence sat on a rock chipping away with handheld hammers at small granite rocks, creating the packing that Noah used to wedge under the large flat boulders. The clink, clink, clinking of the small hammers against the granite stone echoed through the forest. Once in a while, Daniel would get up and help Noah jockey around the larger stones. But the majority of the wall was built by Noah.

Noah was working for a half hour and the foundation of the wall extended ten feet from where Burton had been buried. It was flat and in every respect looked like a level road. Every strike of the handheld sledgehammer that he wielded split the granite stones in just the right places. It was just a matter of Noah placing the split rocks on the wall, as if they were part of a giant jigsaw puzzle. Thor, with his magic hammer, couldn't have done any better.

"That's wonderful, Pa. How do you keep it so straight and level?" Lawrence asked. "It sort of looks like a Roman road that I saw sketched in a book once."

"Yeah," he sighed, stood up, and clapped the stone dust off his gloves and then looked at his work. "That Scottish fella showed my pa, and then my pa showed me. He was a real artist."

Abigail appeared from the forest with an apron filled to the top with blueberries. All at once, after reaching the beginning of the wall and looking down at the work that was done, she suddenly screamed and dropped the berries into the dirt. She put her hands up to her mouth and backed away.

"Abby, what's wrong?" Noah asked. He went over and held her shoulders. Noah came to realize that Abigail had become a lightning rod for everything that was happening recently with the death of Burton.

"Look," she said, as she pointed to the spot where Burton was buried.

The stones that Lawrence put over the grave were moving. They were shifting from underneath. That could mean only one thing to Abigail. Burton was still alive.

"Here, help me," Noah said, as he kneeled down. In a burst of energy, he began pulling off the stones. Lawrence and Daniel helped by clawing at the dirt. The corpse was uncovered at long last and Noah reached in and tore open the shirt. He placed his ear to his chest to listen for a heartbeat. There was none. "He's dead." He looked over in Abigail's direction.

Noah and Lawrence knew all too well what was happening. The body was bloating and swelling up, which made it seem as if the sergeant was still alive. Lawrence saw it in the war, and Noah saw it on the farm with dead animals.

Lawrence got up from the grave and walked over to Abigail and took her in his arms. "Don't worry, Abby, he's dead. We don't have to be afraid of him anymore."

"I'm sorry," she said. "Am I just a silly girl? Tell me the truth."

"No. We weren't too sure ourselves before we dug him up. Here"—he handed her a small hammer—"sit here and help us break into pieces the stones so your dad can build the rest of the wall, and we can get out of here."

The wall started to take shape with the simple method of placing the granite stones—one on two and two on one—until it attained a height of four feet. It was a fence of tightly packed rocks which at first sight would seem to have collapsed without any mortar in between the gaps. But despite all its weight, it still gave the illusion of floating in midair. It was the purist form of craftsmanship because Noah—this simple, hardworking farmer—created harmony out of chaos.

"Pa, can we stop breaking these rocks. It's getting to be boring," Abigail said.

Noah paused for a minute after placing a heavy forty-pound stone on the top of the wall and walked over to where they were producing hearting for the wall.

"Do you know what you're doin' is the most important thing to buildin' the wall?"

"Oh, I didn't know that," Abigail said.

"The littlest chip of stone can hold up a mountain if it's placed in da right place." Then he picked up the hearting, which were spread over the grass and went back to the wall. He looked over his shoulder and said, "All of you can go back to the house, I'm all set."

Daniel and Lawrence harnessed Rebel to the wagon. Lawrence sat in the driver's seat with Abigail sitting next to him and Daniel sitting in the back. Lawrence turned the buckboard toward the road that led to the house. The leather harness squeaked and the chain under the mouth bit jingled as they trotted down the dirt path toward home.

Noah stopped building the wall and watched them leave. He leaned on the wall just above where Burton was buried. He pulled out a small chipped stone that was wedged under a large rock on the wall and flung it into the woods. Then he stared at what he saw as the future of the farm, riding in the buckboard going down the trail to the house.

Even though the outside appearance of Noah Wilson gave the impression that he was rough and unforgiving when it came to the farm, his inner thoughts showed the true man.

They are the hope of the farm whether I like it or not, he thought. I have to let them grow. I have to nourish them and protect them just like I feed my plants to make them grow. I can't pull them up by the roots like a weed. This is one truth that will have to be hidden. With that, he patted the top of the stone wall and continued to place stone upon stone, confident that he was doing the right thing.

10

INTRODUCING
ABBY AND LAWRENCE

WHO ARE THESE two individuals—Abigail and Lawrence? What occupied their time as children and what formed their personalities. These incidents give us a window into these young minds, and if you will, consider it as a metaphor for the rest of their lives. But before we delve into these events, we must know what the day-to-day routine was that demanded their attention.

They got up at 5:00 a.m. to hit the cornfield and finish up harvesting the rest of the corn that had been missed the day before. Sometimes the dew was so thick that the ponchos got rain soaked even though there were no clouds in the starry sky. Later on, as the morning progressed, with a full heart, they greeted the large yellow eye of the sun, burning through the mist that had settled in the valley.

But it was not only corn that they picked, there also was a cornucopia of other vegetables—the red and green peppers, the black eggplant, the yellow and green squash, the small patch of tomatoes, potatoes, onions, and finally, the purple cabbage.

All the produce was brought into the big red barn—a barn that Noah's neighbors helped him build. Each piece was washed and sorted, and either wrapped up to be transported and sold elsewhere or put in baskets to be sold locally.

The produce gave off their own individual odors; the tomatoes held on to an acidy garden smell, the purple cabbage had a sharp gaseous odor, and the apples had a cinnamon sweet smell to them. The onions had a pungent savory scent, and they overpowered the rest of the crops. But overall, the barn was filled with a light sweet smell indicating that the food that they had picked was ready.

The fresh, ripe vegetables were tightly formed with round sensuous curves and colors. The surfaces were consistent and unblemished. Firm, crisp, and plump were the words that guided the children's selections. They ran their fingers over the velvety smooth skins of the peppers and tomatoes.

Because it was too important to leave the children alone to do the selection, Noah at first would hang around supervising the operation, but it soon became apparent that the children knew exactly what they were doing so he attended to other chores that had to be finished.

There was respect for the harvest. Not once in the whole time that they sorted the yield did they throw a rotten tomato at each other or complain about the work. They talked and laughed and worked.

They worked nonstop, or until the snow stopped them from getting out of the house. When it was possible again, they went back to a schedule of planting, weeding, watering, and harvesting into the late spring to late fall.

The rest of the year, they prepared the land by turning it in late fall and early winter and planting seeds in the colder months. And so it went year after year on the farm. It was a tradition that was handed down from generation to generation, from father to son.

Noah was determined to pass that tradition on to Lawrence and Abigail. He knew that it took more than blood connection to tie a person to the farm. It took hard work, faith, and love. This is what he hoped these young adopted children learned as they grew up on the farm and that they carried those values with them.

The Wilson farm was an Eden in the midst of war. And there were mysteries galore to find if you only looked. It was one of the advantages of being a farmer in the North.

After the pastor dropped off Lawrence at the farm so that Noah could raise him, Noah said, "Look around Lawrence"—he held him by his shoulders—"this is your new home." And then he pulled him close and hugged him. "I'm sorry to hear about your parents. Abigail is around some place, I think she's in the orchard picking apples, look around."

While he explored the new farm, he was greeted with a squadron of dragonflies dive-bombing him from behind. The buzz of their wings resonated in his ears. There was life under every step. He walked through the field of corn that was parallel to the apple orchard. And after a while, he absentmindedly found himself in the forest because the thought of not seeing his parents ever again weighed heavy on his mind so he wandered, not aware about where he was going.

He squished a pokeweed, crushing the purple berries, staining the gummy bottoms of his high-top leather shoes. In the distance, through the trees, he saw a black shape nestled in a low-lying apple tree. He rubbed his eyes and squinted as hard as he could.

He jumped over an old stone wall which brought him parallel to the squirming black outline. "My god, it's a bear," he whispered to himself.

He squatted below a low-lying apple branch that almost touched the ground, sweating, hoping the black bear didn't hear the loud frightened thump of his heart.

It was lounging in the arms of the old apple tree that was covered with blueberry vines and overgrown with brush. Every so often, it would nibble apples from the tree or berries from the vine.

Lawrence was totally absorbed in the sight of the black hairy bear in the tree when suddenly he felt a hand on his shoulder. He jumped into the air, turned around, and came face-to-face with a nine-year-old tomboy. She was a little bit shorter than him.

"Hi, my name is Abigail," she said. The girl was dressed in overall jeans. She also had on a peach-colored shirt, a floppy brown canvas hat, and a pair of ladies boots.

"My name is Lawrence." He bent over, put his hands on his thighs, trying to catch his breath as his heart beat hard against his chest. "Gee, I almost peed in my pants," he said. "Give a guy a warning."

"Oh, I'm sorry." She looked over his head at the bear in the tree. It appeared to Lawrence that she was comfortable and familiar with her surroundings.

Lawrence pulled her down in one motion as he rested his back against the trunk of the apple tree. "Stay down," he whispered. "The bear will see us."

"Oh, don't worry, that's just Cleopatra. She won't bother us. She's just a lazy-bone." Then she started to get up again. But Lawrence pulled her back down again.

All of a sudden, the bear growled and vocalized with woofs, snorts, and jaw popping as it charged. Lawrence at once started running, grabbing a hold of Abigail, and pulling her in the direction of the toolshed right through a flock of turkey vultures that were gorging themselves on the rotten apples on the ground. They flapped up and away more surprised than Lawrence as he ran through the middle of them.

"Don't run, it's okay," she shouted, as she was being pulled along behind Lawrence. But the bear did not stop. "Yikes," she screamed as she looked back.

They ended up in the shack looking at the bear through the window as it sniffed and blew at the toolshed door.

"Wow, that was close," Lawrence said. The sweat from his forehead plopped onto the window sill.

"Cleo never did that before," Abigail said as she flopped hard onto a pile of burlap bags. She covered her face with her floppy hat.

"You got any matches?" Lawrence asked. He started to rummage around the shed, moving shovels and rakes so that the clang of the tools rang in their ears.

"No," she said, flipping the brim of the hat off her face.

"That's okay, I got what I need." He found a small box of wood matches under the shovel. He took an apple branch three feet long and scraped off the bark on one end with a hook knife he had found. Next, he picked up some oil-soaked rags lying next to the saw and wrapped them around the stick. And then, he tied the rags up. He wound the old piece of cloth around the stick over and over again.

"What are you doing?" Abigail asked as she got up.

"You'll see." Then he struck a wood match, lit the torch, shoved open the door, and walked out with it in his hand. The bear sprinted away down the path, disappearing into the woods.

"You're my hero," she said, while she held both her hands together, put them up to her cheek, and batted her eyes.

"Thanks," he said with a forced trembling half smile and a hard swallow.

"What do we do now?"

"Let's go up to that cave up there. That's probably where Cleopatra lives," Lawrence breathed fast and started to run down the orchard.

"Are you crazy? We just got rid of her," Abigail shouted.

He stopped and turned around. "It'll be all right. Just follow me," he said. "She's roaming around in the woods."

"Get in back of me. I'll lead the way." He hesitated. *I hope I'm right*, he thought. He looked left, right, and ahead as they ran down the aisles of apple trees with the torch held high above his head. It had become dark by now. He thought that he was like Columbus, exploring a new world.

"It's up here." He pointed to a cave in the elbow of the cliff.

Now that they were in front of the opening, he could see a carpet of green plume moss at its entrance. He thrust the torch into the opening and slipped his head in next to the light. The inside of the cave felt cool, compared to the hot July sun outside. Pushing the burning stick to one side, he crawled in on his belly.

"Come on," he said. He looked over his shoulder for Abigail.

At last, he stood up, grabbed the torch, held it high above his head, and surveyed the new world. Looking up, he saw a large granite room twelve feet high, fifteen feet wide and stretching out in front of him into the darkness.

"This is wonderful?" Abigail said as she crawled through the opening, clapping the dirt from her hands and off her knees as she got to her feet.

Lawrence warily looked back at the cave entrance. "I hope that Cleo doesn't come back to soon," he said. Next to the opening, he saw a pile of leaves, grass, and rotted wood that looked like a nest or bed.

"No. I don't think so," Abigail said, looking toward the entrance with wide eyes and the sound of trepidation in her voice.

As it happened, the light from the torch startled a flock of bats as they squeaked and clicked, making for a hole in the roof of the cave. Lawrence and Abigail backed up to the wall.

After a few moments, they walked over to a small pool fed by a stream coming through an opening in the rocks. The deep and quiet water had colorless, blind crawfish darting around in the bottom. The moving bright spots in the water were the eyes of the crawfish, shining like cat's eyes, reflecting the light of the fire.

"I've never seen anything like that in my life," Lawrence said as he stepped back with raised eyebrows. Then he bent down closer to the water.

"What are they, Lawrence?" Abigail asked.

"You telling me you don't know!" Lawrence put the torch close to Abigail's face.

With a slight shrug of her shoulders, she said, "No. It's the first time I've ever been in this cave. I didn't know Cleopatra lived in here. There would be days when I wouldn't see her in the orchard at all."

Lawrence's mouth went dry, and his legs became rubbery. He wanted to push deeper into the cave, but he was afraid of Cleopatra coming back to her den. He grabbed Abigail's hand and pulled her along, feeling the nervous sweat from her hand mingle with his.

The farther he went, the more he heard the sound of faint peeping, and the clatter of tiny feet, like mice walking over glass.

"Look at that," Lawrence said, holding the torch higher above his head.

A pack rat's nest made of twigs; pine boughs and black bear's hair was above and to the left. The little mouse-like creatures were building their home.

All of a sudden, they heard shuffling and intense grunting coming from the entrance of the cave, then the sound of deep sniffing and blowing. It was the bear.

"What do we do now?" Abigail asked, the fear coming out in her trembling voice.

Lawrence looked at the cave entrance. "Maybe we could just run by her real fast and out the door. No, we still have to crawl by her. It would never work"—he put out the fire and thought that there had to be another way out—"let's look around."

"There, Lawrence, there's an opening," Abigail whispered, pointing to a hole in the back of the cave just above the pack rat's home.

"You're right. It's the way in for the mouse," he said, poking the stick through the hole to make it big enough to fit all the way through, "You go first."

"Thanks," Abigail pulled the loose rocks out of the way, tore off her hat and poked her head through the hole, and then squeezed her shoulders through. She had only gotten halfway out.

"Get going. I can hear Cleo coming," he shouted.

By now, Abigail had made it out. And Lawrence popped through the hole just behind her, but his legs were still in the cave. He felt something pulling at his foot. Just as he pulled himself out, his shoe dropped back in the opening. They stood still in the dark looking back down into the hole, at the same time, letting out a sigh of relief.

Those hugs he ached for from his deceased mother and father did not seem as important to him anymore. The excitement of this new world, for the moment, was all he needed.

11

DANIEL IN THE LION'S DEN

LAWRENCE PULLED UP in between a field of corn on one side and a field of ripening tomatoes on the other.

"Drop us off here, Abby," he said while handing her the reins. "Come on, Daniel, let's pick some baskets of vegetables before it gets dark."

"Yes, Mista' Lawrence," Daniel said. Then he slid himself off the end of the buckboard and went into the tomato field.

Even before Lawrence got settled in the field, Daniel was picking tomatoes and filling the willow baskets to overflowing. He piled them in a row next to the dirt trail. *I remember when they said that tomatoes were poisonous, but people seem to love them now*, he thought. The fruit had peculiar names attached to them—Abraham Lincoln, Brandywine, Mortgage Lifter, Great White Beefsteak, Cherokee Purple, and Ruffled Yellow. The shapes were flat and some of the skins had a pleated texture.

Lawrence hobbled to the road. "Hey, Daniel," he hollered. "Slow down, will ya? You're making me look bad."

Daniel, hearing Lawrence, turned right away and whooshed through the bushy tomato plants, stepping with care around them to finally stand where Lawrence could see him. "Whad you say, Mista' Lawrence?" Daniel asked.

"I've got to show Noah that I can pull my own weight. He thinks because I've got a bum leg that I can't do my chores. Slow down. I can't keep up."

He's just another white soldier boy. Why should I help him? Daniel thought. Even though the Wilsons have treated me like one of the family, I have a hard time forgetting about the beatings I used to get when I was a boy in South Carolina. A hard time forgetting how that white boss man marked up my back with his whip. He whipped out my feelings of hope and forgiveness.

But these people are different. *Maybe I can let my guard down*, he thought. "Okay, Mista' Lawrence. I'll tell you what I'll do. I'll pick just as fast as before 'cause it wouldn't be fair to Noah for me to slow up, but I'll tell him that you picked most of the tomatoes."

"Is that a bluff?" Lawrence asked.

"Nope."

Lawrence flipped over a basket and sat on it hard. "Thanks, Daniel. You're a good man." He took in a deep breath and smiled.

"Okay," Daniel said. After that, he turned back into the field and began again snapping off the tomatoes and dropping them into the baskets.

In the back of the farm was a road—not used very much now—that snaked along the stream past the stone walls and came out on the side of small tomato field. During the war, the road was used a lot for repositioning troops down South or for moving cannons and supplies to the railhead.

However now, it was used for a more insidious purpose. Before, northerners got the bad reputation of pillaging the South and were being called carpetbaggers. They used this road to go to those southern states that were too weak to defend themselves, so they could take advantage of the chaos. With this purpose in mind, a ragtag group of men stopped along the path and began stealing corn and tomatoes from the fields.

The sun was setting on the horizon and dark shadows began to appear in the forest. Daniel could see torches coming through the woods and hear the sound of what he thought was a small wagon and horses coming down the road. He ran over to the narrow road. The horses were chestnut, black, and gray. The clothes they wore were a combination of a Union soldier's uniform and civilian clothes.

And the man who led the procession was seated on a white horse and still had a captain's uniform on, with the distinctive chicken guts on his shoulders. His hat had the brim pinned up on one side with peacock feathers peeking out from under a gold pin.

Every man was busy stealing as much corn and cucumbers and summer squash that they could get their hands on. They threw everything into the back of the small covered wagon.

"Hey, you no-account men, put that stuff back," Daniel shouted. Just as Daniel yelled, he realized the mistake he made.

The officer withdrew his sword and whirled it in the air and said, "Grab that contraband slave, men. He'll be worth a lot of money down South."

"I'm not contraband," Daniel said as two soldiers grabbed him and pushed him toward the forest.

They tied him to a tree, and then they gagged him. One of the soldiers said, "There you go, Uncle Tom." Daniel felt helpless as he struggled with the ropes, trying to get loose. They cut deep into his skin.

What happened next, Daniel could hardly believe. Lawrence came hopping through the field headed for the thieves. When he saw the hornets' nest that he got himself into, he came to a skidding halt. *How he could be so stupid*, Daniel thought.

Suddenly, every Springfield rifle was aimed at Lawrence's head.

"Well, well, what do we have here?" the officer asked. "Seems like a toddling, Sunday soldier."

"I'm not a Sunday soldier," Lawrence said. I was in the war. That's where I got this." He pointed to his foot.

"Well then, you won't mind sitting down and taking a rest for a while," the officer said. "Tie him up and gag him too." They sat Lawrence down on a rock next to Daniel. Daniel stared down at Lawrence and shook his head and scrunched up his shoulders to show his hopelessness.

By now, darkness swallowed up the forest. And the only movement was by those animals that roamed at night. These soldiers were just those kinds of animals. The silence of the nighttime was disturbed by these thieves talking loud and scurrying through the blackness with no regard to the sanctity of the woods. They were in a frenzy to grab as much as they could in as little time as they could.

Suddenly, Daniel felt somebody trying to undo the ropes around his wrists. And everything in the forest was quiet again because the ragtag soldiers were finished taking their fill. He could feel the handle of a pistol in his hand. "Wait till I cut the rest of the ropes before you use the gun," Noah whispered.

Daniel saw that Lawrence relaxed his arms that were tight in back of him. His ropes were cut. He was loose and had a gun in his hand. Even with the gag in his mouth, a slight smile came to the corner of his lips, and then he winked at Daniel.

"Okay, fellas, that's it," Noah hollered. After that, he fired one of the barrels of the double-barreled shotgun.

The boom of the gun echoed through the night. Lawrence stood up and ripped the gag out of his mouth and then pointed the gun at the thieves. Daniel did the same.

Daniel held his head and body erect. In his whole life, he never pointed a gun at a white man, especially a white soldier man. He was puffed up with pride. *When, till now, had life been so good to him?* he thought. It felt good to be part of the solution instead of being told all your life that you were part of the problem. He stood shoulder to shoulder with Lawrence and Noah defending the farm that he loved so much.

"Stay where ya are," Noah said, while he walked to the back of the covered wagon, all the while pointing the shotgun at the officer on the white horse. "You get it first if ya decide to light out. Understand?"

"Okay, pilgrim," the officer said.

Noah walked to the back of the small wagon and pulled back the white canvas cover. "How many of ya are there?" he asked.

"Oh...I don't know ten of us, I suppose," the officer said. "Why?"

"I think ya could make out pretty well with only half of what you've got in the back of his wagon." Then he walked back to the officer and pointed the shotgun directly at his chest. "Now tell your men to put half of what you stole back in the baskets that I have stacked up at the end of the road."

"Whatever you say, boss," the officer said. "Do what he says, men." The soldiers were trained well. And in a couple of minutes, half of what they had stolen was put back in baskets at the end of the road.

"Skedaddle out of here and don't let me see ya on my farm again," Noah said. He waved the shotgun in the air.

As Daniel watched the robbers leave, he noticed that they turned around many times to see if possibly Noah was going to shoot them in the back. This more than anything else showed Daniel their true colors. Only men like that could think that somebody would do such a thing, because that's exactly what they would have done.

It occurred to him, after what had just happened, that there were different kinds of white men. The contrast was so stark that it changed Daniel's thinking, and he could feel the hatred melting away.

Noah leaned on a white birch tree as he watched the procession of soldiers fade into the darkness of the night and go over the hill out of sight.

After he was sure that the thieves were gone, he swung the shotgun over his shoulder and turned back to face the men. "Let's go home, boys," he said. "It's been quite an interesting few days since you came back, Lawrence."

"Yeah, I know what you mean, Pa. It's almost like being back in the war."

"Guess we have to be on our guard to protect what's important to us, even when there is no war," Daniel said. He could see what he said affected Noah and Lawrence. It covered them, it changed how they walked, and it trickled into their minds so they would never be the same again.

The three men walked down the road side by side, being guided by a lantern in the distance that was hung off the barn to light their way home.

12

BLACKMAIL

THE SUN CAME up warming the air and reaching down into the soil caressing it, encouraging it, and giving it life. The rain followed on the heels of the morning sun which quenched the soils thirst. It gave drink to everything it touched. It even seeped down into the makeshift grave that held Burton's body, washing it clean of any sins. It was an eternal cycle of death and rebirth.

An uneventful week went by on the farm with chores to do and plants to tend. But now there was an atmosphere of uneasiness that followed everybody around—a dark shadow of guilt that never let go.

Not only the ghosts of war plagued these people on the farm, but the apparition of the soldier buried in the ground—Noah's hallowed ground—also oozed up through the soil and infected all their lives.

Many times, Lawrence and Abigail passed by each other not saying a word, afraid to look in each other's eyes, anxious that they would see the dead body reflected in the mirror of their minds.

Even Noah passing by the wall, while riding the buckboard out to the fields, had a feeling of foreboding. The premonition scratched at his sense of right and wrong. *This is like cholera passing on its disease to everybody on my farm*, he thought. *But what else can I do.*

Then, one afternoon, while the weather outside was sending sheets of rain on the roof and rattling the windows in the parlor, Abigail was trying to get around Lawrence in the narrow pantry. She had a pile of dishes in her arms.

"We have to talk, Abby," Lawrence said. He held her tight against his upper body, squashing her and the dishes close to him. He smelled the essence of her, although it was more than that, it was her aura—fresh, clean, young—and it made his heart beat hard against his chest. But under all that young freshness, he smelled the hint of the homemade whiskey that he made. "Did you have some of my whiskey? I can smell it on your breath."

"Just a little. I saw your still in the barn, and I just had to try it. Just enough to calm my nerves," she said. "Is that all right? I only took a sip of the rotten stuff, not even enough to fill a thimble." But the way she staggered in his arms and tried to steady herself told Lawrence the truth. It was more than a thimble full.

"It's okay. You can have everything I've got," he said. "But most of all, I'd like to give you my heart, but I've been noticing that I can't even get close to you." He was eager for her to have a reaction to what he said, but it was as if she was deaf to any kindness or humor.

"Let me get by, Lawrence," she said. She tried to squeeze through, but he held her even tighter. The dishes clinked and squealed against each other in her arms.

He kissed her full on the mouth, and the dishes crashed to the floor. Their shattering sound ran up Lawrence's spine until his whole body shuttered and then little by little calmed down. They stood in a pile of white broken plates.

"What are we doing to each other, Abby?" he asked, looking down at her.

"Yes, I know. I have been avoiding you. I couldn't look at you anymore. I was ashamed," she said.

"Are you going to let Burton's death ruin our lives?" He reached down and pulled her chin up off his chest. For the first time in a long time, they gazed at each other with tears in their eyes.

"No," she said.

"Then let's get married like we planned," he said.

"You still want to marry me after what I did?" She backed up so she could get a better look at his face. "I'm seventeen going on eighteen, you know. I was afraid I was going to be an old maid if you didn't talk to Pa and ask me to get married soon."

"I still want to marry you so you won't become an old maid," he said. He smiled at her as he drank in her naive innocence. "I was there too, you know. I'm just as responsible for what happened as you are."

Lawrence noticed that all the tension drained from Abigail's face, and a smile began to creep across her lips. When she stepped back into his arms, he became aware of the muscles in her back and shoulders relaxing as her smile got bigger and bigger. Then all of a sudden, as if she had come back to life, she began to get excited about the wedding. Their love began again.

"I have to start to send out the invitations. I have to tell Pa. I have to get my dress, oh no, I have a dress. You have to get all the men together. Get the preacher, the food. We have plenty of food."

He kissed her on the forehead and then said, "You go and take care of what has to be taken care of, and I'll pick up the broken dishes." For the first time in a week, Lawrence was feeling good about their relationship. Now he thought that we might have a chance. He could hear her in the bedroom just above the pantry, moving furniture and opening and closing trunks.

"Don't worry about anything, Lawrence," she hollered down from upstairs. "You just show up."

Lawrence walked over to the railing that led upstairs and grabbed a hold of it and hollered up into the darkness. "The rain stopped. I'm going out to the field to help Daniel."

A faint voice came through the middle of all the clatter and scraping from upstairs. "Okay...okay," she said in a frenzied tone.

He shook his head and snickered while walking back into the kitchen. He was happy that Abigail was excited about the wedding and he knew that all the preparations for the big day would keep her mind occupied. "Ooh—he grabbed hold of the kitchen chair—that hurts," he said to himself. Ever since the time he had gotten his foot run over it turned into a barometer. It ached when it was going to rain or storm and kept hurting until the thunderstorm went away.

He limped out to the barn and put the bridle in Rebel's mouth and then jumped from a bale of hay onto his back. He was late going out to the field to help Daniel with the picking. The beautiful summer day raised his spirits. The sun streamed through the trees, and the little sparrows darted through the corn. It appeared to Lawrence that Rebel was even affected by his surroundings, since he sidestepped and reared his head trotting down the dirt road.

The rain was over and steam was coming off the fields. It made Lawrence sweat and squirm in his clothes to get a more comfortable position on the horse's back because it was slippery. He wiped the perspiration from his brow.

Daniel should be in the six-foot-high cornfield, but he's nowhere to be found, Lawrence thought. "Daniel, where are you?" Lawrence hollered. He went into the field atop of Rebel, stretching up high to give him some advantage. "Danny boy, are you in here?" The brown stalks of corn, baked in the sun, were already picked clean. Daniel should have been harvesting what was available in the middle of the tall green plants, but there was no trace of him. Lawrence went into the field crackling through the aisles of plants looking through the openings. At first, Lawrence thought that Daniel was sleeping somewhere in the field but dismissed that thought knowing the kind of man he was. He started to get worried.

He plowed through the pasture, but he was nowhere to be found. Then he traveled back toward the barn and rode into the building. He looked up into the loft and into the stalls. "Daniel, are you in here?" he hollered. There was no answer.

After that, he went toward the pump and ended up on the road that passed by the front of the farmhouse. He sat for a while next to the street feeling frustrated and frowning. His eyes were cast downward steadily since his mind was trying to figure out where his friend could be.

All of a sudden, he heard a muffled tapping coming from the root cellar. Without delay, he slipped off Rebel and went over and pulled open the door. Daniel was tied up hand and foot with a gag in his mouth.

"Who did this to you?" Lawrence asked, pulling the gag out of his mouth.

"Those white soldier men did this," Daniel said. He untied the ropes and threw them to the back of the cellar.

"Are they the same people that we chased away about a week ago?" Lawrence asked.

"Yes, sir, that's them." When they left, they bent down to avoid bumping their heads as they came out of the cellar.

"Come on. Let's get out of here." Lawrence stepped on a rock and boosted himself up on the horse's back, and then he reached down and lifted Daniel up on to the back of the horse. They started to leave but were stopped when a gang of men came out of the forest, looking like ghosts. They pointed their Springfield rifles at them as soon as the huge crowd slithered through the wild blackberry and sweetbriar bushes.

The captain, John Webb, came out right behind them. His brass buttons gleamed in the sun as well as the hilt of his Calvary officer's sword. "Well, I see somebody is trying to take my property," he said as he pulled out his sword and used it like a pointer.

"He's not property, he's Daniel," Lawrence said.

"Oh, the Sunday soldier speaks up," the captain said. "He belongs to you?"

"No. He's his own man. He doesn't belong to anybody."

"No? You're wrong, he belongs to me."

"Let's get out of here, Daniel," Lawrence said as he pulled on the reins in an effort to get by. Daniel tightened his grip around Lawrence's stomach. All at once, the soldiers closed in on them. Lawrence thought he heard a low growl come from the men, like mad dogs ready to pounce. He could feel Daniel shaking with fear behind him.

"It's okay, men," the captain said, "We'll, let 'em think about it for a while."

"What do you want?" Lawrence asked.

"It would be a shame to have that beautiful barn burn down or have your well contaminated," the captain said.

"I get the idea. So what do you want?" Lawrence leered at the officer. In his mind's eye, he saw himself grabbing the sword and running him through with it.

The captain had a devilish grin on his face. He leaned on the horn of the saddle and stroked his chin. "I'll tell you what I'll do. Since you don't have any greenbacks, you can pay me for my property by leaving twenty baskets of produce in the forest next to that newly built wall in the north pasture every week. I'll tell you when you can stop."

"Do I have a choice?" Lawrence asked.

"Nope," the captain said. "Maybe you don't realize how valuable that produce is down South now. It's like baskets of gold. People will pay high prices for food."

To add to the troubles that the people had in the South that summer, they also had the burden that in many states there was a severe drought. Even if they had the seeds to grow crops, which they didn't, they still needed the rain to grow their produce.

"Okay, you got a deal," Lawrence said. Because he thought the talk was over, he tried to go through the line of soldiers blocking his way, but they stood fast.

"It's all right, boys, let 'em go," the captain said. "You remember what I told you." Then he put his sword back in the scabbard.

"I will," Lawrence said as he rode away.

Daniel talked in Lawrence's ear while they rode back to the fields. "Mista' Lawrence, it's better we go to the law and tell 'em what's goin' on with those men," he said.

"We can't. They might find out about us burying Burton under the wall," Lawrence said.

"Oh yeah, I plum forgot about that," Daniel said. "Boy, we is in a pickle."

While they rode back to the fields, disturbing thoughts were running through Lawrence's mind. *We have to pick twice as much as we did before*, he thought. I don't know if I can keep up. I don't know if even Daniel can pick that much. I needed him. I had to do it.

It's a cruel irony that we have to put all the produce right next to Burton's grave. *It is as if we were bringing food for the gods for the sacrifice that was buried under the wall*, Lawrence thought. It made Lawrence clench his jaw, and his palms began to sweat. The anxiety turned a switch on in his brain that made him hear the ghosts of war.

He pulled hard on the reins of the horse making it rear up, dumping Daniel and him off onto the ground.

"Can you hear the cannons and the crack of the muskets?" Lawrence asked Daniel.

"No, Mista' Lawrence, I don't hear noting," Daniel said. All at once, he ran over and held tight on to Rebel's bridle. His eyes and mouth opened wide, and his eyebrows rose since he had never seen Lawrence so upset.

Lawrence dropped to his knees and then sat back on his heels. "I'm sorry, Danny. I didn't mean to scare you." He stood up and shook his head and took in a deep breath. "You look like you saw a ghost. I'm all right now."

Daniel laced his fingers together, and Lawrence stepped into his hands and then he lifted him up and onto the horse. "Let's start picking, Daniel," Lawrence said, talking down to him at the same time as he walked beside the horse. "I'm worried about the tally that we have to keep up with. We better get going."

"That's a good idea, boss. We better get busy," Daniel said. Lawrence marveled at Daniel's skill. He had barely gotten off the horse when he noticed that Daniel had one basket full and was half done with the second.

Lawrence let out a deep sigh of relief and then tied Rebel to a nearby white birch tree.

They worked till dusk until they could barely see what they were picking. "Let's call it a day, Daniel," Lawrence said. "It's too dark."

"Okay, Mista' Lawrence. I feel a lot more tired than I usually feel," Daniel said. "Just got some crampin' in my legs, and my stomach don't feel so good."

The next day, Lawrence called up to Daniel's room. "Daniel…Daniel, it's time to get to work," he hollered. But he did not answer. Noah came to the head of the stairs.

"Lawrence, Daniel's got the cholera," he shouted. "I told 'em not to drink the water coming out of the stream, ta drink only the pump water, but he didn't listen ta me."

"Give him some hickory bark tea. Is it real bad?" Lawrence asked.

"I don't know yet," Noah said. "I'm giving him some laudanum. It seems to help." Then he turned back toward the room.

"Okay, Pa," Lawrence said. He felt as if a mule had kicked him in the stomach.

Lawrence picked the vegetables the best he could. He pushed along a small wooden cart down the narrow aisles of corn, sometimes sitting on it resting and other times picking right from the little handcart, kneeling with his damaged foot hanging limp on the opposite side.

If it wasn't for the backbreaking work, Lawrence would have enjoyed it. When he was in the army between the lulls in the fighting, there were times when he had trouble being alone with his thoughts. There was always something doing. Privacy was a rare commodity in the midst of all those men.

But in spite of the tally of produce that had to be made and Daniel becoming sick, Lawrence took advantage of the solitude. He would linger in the fields past sundown and look up at the stars. As he concentrated on those silver pinpoints of light, he had the sensation of being lifted out of himself, and the thought of war, and everything connected to it faded away. His stomach lifted into his expanding heart, his breathing got deeper, and his chest filled with life. As he focused his eyes on the cloud of stars in the summer sky, he felt his body lose all its weight, and he fell off into a deep sleep.

When he woke and saw the milky cloud rolling into the western sky, he thought how the Greeks of long ago saw this spectacle. They believed that all the celestial objects— the moon, the sun, and the stars—rose out of a universal ocean in the east and dipped into the sea in the west. It was one of the only times that he was free of the ghosts of war.

Even though his mind could escape once in a while, his task was still Herculean, and it drained every strength that he had. Many times, when it started to get dark and the sound of the crickets chirped in his ears, Lawrence would fall asleep again and again on the little cart and wake up to a starry night. He would walk back at a snail's pace to the farmhouse, dragging the little cart behind him. But he knew what had to be done and the dire consequences if he failed to fill the tally.

13

WISDOM OF CROWDS

DANIEL HAD GOTTEN better, Abigail had prepared for the wedding, and Noah braced his farm for the invasion of all the people who were invited to the gathering and even for the people who weren't. All of Noah's relations were invited. And an attempt was made to invite the long lost relatives of Lawrence and Abigail, as difficult as that might be.

The guests arrived in the early morning for the wedding, on foot, in one horse trap, and on horseback. It was becoming a scene of bedlam with all the unfamiliar people coming from miles around, pouring into the little farm with only Lawrence, Daniel, and Noah to police the crowds.

Lawrence stopped as many people as he could and shook their hands. He reached up to the people on horseback; he stopped carriages and reached through the leather curtains. "Welcome to our day," he said. "We hope you have a good time."

A large family of ten children and their two parents came trudging up the small path next to the house. There were six boys and four girls. The little boys, ages five to eight, wore long trousers, boots, and double-breasted pullover shirts. One of the boys had red, white, and blue suspenders on. The two youngest boys had sailor's suits on, and Lawrence had to bend in half to shake their hands. "Hello, little seaman," Lawrence said.

The boy turned to his father and asked, "What's a seaman, Papa?"

The boy's father, dressed in a waist coat with a black top hat on, said, "That's a good thing, Ezra."

"Oh," he said. Then he thanked Lawrence and moved on.

Parasols, bonnets, fans, broaches, and cloaks were some of the first things that caught the eye when you looked into the crowd.

Lawrence turned to the young girls. Most of the girls looked like they came out of *Godey's Lady's Book,* a fashion magazine. Their dresses had tightly fitting bodices that rode low on the shoulder and had a V-shaped neckline. "You look lovely, girls," he said. They were dressed in gingham dresses and had on close bonnets of purple, or bonnets of black velvet, turned up in front on their heads and held bouquets of wild flowers in their hands. They giggled and covered their mouths and congregated on the side of the summer kitchen. There, they preened themselves. They reminded him of kittens licking their fur.

The mother had a gown on that was tightly cinched around the waist, and she held a colorful parasol shading her from the sun. A cabriolet bonnet with a flaring brim hid some of her face. She and her husband walked arm in arm.

Lawrence had his Union cap on, took off his hat, and made a sweeping bow. "Welcome, madam," he said.

They both stopped. "Thank you," she said.

The man tipped his hat. From the way he held himself, straight and rigid, Lawrence could see that he was a strict disciplinarian. "Who did you fight with, soldier?" he asked.

"Connecticut, First Battery Light Artillery," Lawrence said. Then he put his hat back on and watched as the couple went into the farmhouse.

Some people came from thirty miles away, from Seymour, New Haven, and Bridgeport. And one couple, as soon as they saw Lawrence, came over and hugged him. The man was dressed in Levi's jeans and the women had on a walking dress. "Hi, my name is Dale Comstock, and this is my wife Martha," Suddenly, they backed away. "Don't you recognize us, Lawrence?" Lawrence stepped back stiff and defensive. They made him feel like he was their son, which was a sensation that he had forgotten after his parents died and which they brought back when they embraced him.

"No, I'm afraid you have me at a disadvantage, sir," Lawrence said.

"We knew your parents when you were only three or four before you came to live with Abigail and Noah."

Lawrence looked at the couple long and hard, trying to remember back to his childhood. Slowly, a grin came over his face and then it grew into a smile that reached from ear to ear, then he began to laugh. "Now I remember you, Dale. But most of all, I remember your handlebar mustache tickling me when I got close to your cheek." Somehow, when he talked to the couple, he experienced a rush of emotion as if he was talking to his deceased parents. He wondered if his dead mom and dad were hugging him through Dale and Martha.

The couple laughed. "That's right. Now you got it," he said. "I see you got a war wound, Lawrence?"

"Yeah, it's not so bad. I know other soldiers a lot worse off than me."

"That's the spirit. Never say die," he said and then patted Lawrence on the shoulder. "We'll see you later." They disappeared into the crowd of people. Lawrence watched them as they walked away and how Martha, his wife, stuck close by his side, matching his every step so they appeared to be one person, just like his parents used to do. He only hoped that he and Abigail would be as inseparable.

The Comstocks were from a saner time in his life before the war, a time before all the hurt.

A farm wagon came, rumbling up the road. It seemed to be filled with what was a mountain family. Lawrence had never seen them before. The young men had on floppy hats and were dressed in unkempt overalls. The rifles were out-of-date, and they cradled them against their chests lovingly, as if they were the newest Springfields made. The father had bear crease on his hair to keep it down on his head.

They stopped right in front of Lawrence. "Here, son, take a swig of this," the father said as he leaned down from the wagon and put a brown porcelain jug in front of Lawrence. His hair smelled of a "cooked" grease odor when he passed the jug.

"Thank you, sir," Lawrence said. "I'm sure it's a fine mash whiskey." Lawrence took a long drink from the jug, tipping it up and resting it on his shoulder, sucking it into his mouth. It smelled pungent and sharp, making his eyes water. It tasted crisp, going directly through his pallet into his bloodstream. He coughed and tried to regain his breath then wiped off the rest of the whiskey from his mouth onto his sleeve. "That's smooth," Lawrence said. Of course, he was lying, but these were his guests, and he felt it was his responsibility to make them feel at home. Their homemade concoction was worse than his.

"We're the McCoys," the old man said. "Thanks for invitin' us." Then, the daughter, who Lawrence thought was too young to be in control of the two big draft horses that were pulling the wagon, snapped the reins across the horse's rump. They ended up leaving it next to the barn, jumping out of the farm wagon, and heading toward the farmhouse. It seemed to Lawrence that this group of people was used to taking their rifles into their houses because they strolled into the summer kitchen and then into the living room with their weapons under their arms.

There happened to be a lull in the greetings and that was when Lawrence became aware of a sense of joy welling up in his chest when he saw all his comrades from the war gallop up from the road and stop in front of him.

They were brothers in arms and understood every agony and happiness that resided in his heart because everything that he went through, they experienced too. *They went through Camp Tyler in Hanover, Connecticut, just like I did*, he thought. They were all virgins once, long ago, just like me. And while he watched them pull up in front of him, he understood that they were unaware of the horrors of war once, just like he was but now they knew better. But he wondered why they didn't come back with the phantoms of war still in their dreams like he did.

There was Sam Carpenter, the oldest of the soldiers; Oliver Flood, the boy he taught to read like Abigail taught him; Charlie Jillson, the first recruit he met when he went to camp; and Eddie Johnson, the guy who always chewed tobacco.

Eddie's horse slid up to the porch, popping him up off his saddle. He held tight on to the horn so he would not be catapulted off into the overhang. "Hey, Lawrence, want a chaw?" He asked as he leaned down and shoved a square piece into Lawrence's face. Then he spit a brown spray of tobacco into the dust. He could hear the splat of the liquid tobacco hit the ground.

"No thanks, Ed," Lawrence said.

"Ah, go ahead. You'll like it."

Lawrence took a hunk off the little bar of tobacco by sticking it in his back teeth and tearing off a small piece. It smelled musty and had a burnt taste.

They were all dressed in the typical cavalry uniform—blue jacket, guilt buttons, black leather belts. light-blue breeches, leather boots, and blue forage caps. The horses trotted in place excited about being alive. They smelled fragrant as the combination of their natural sweat combined with the animal hide smell of the leather saddles. It also brought back memories of the tack room in camp. The leather had a sweet oily aroma to it.

Then Charlie Jillson's horse sauntered up. His left arm had been amputated, and the sleeve was pinned up on his shoulder. "Hey, General, how are you doing?" he asked.

Lawrence walked up to him and squeezed his boot. "Can't complain," he said. Then Lawrence spit the rest of the tobacco into his hand and tossed it on the ground. He never got the habit of chewing tobacco, even though everybody around him was chomping and spitting every chance they got.

"You got out of the army only to be drafted into another army," Charlie said.

Everybody laughed. "No it's not like that. She's sweet and kind." He stroked Charlie's horse and looked down at the ground. He became aware that he was blushing, so he turned his head away so they wouldn't notice the emotion that came across his face. "Besides ,we grew up together."

Every now and then, the neighing of a horse or the laughter of all the people in the house could be heard. Many horses that were tied to the side of the barn were getting annoyed and eager to be doing something instead of being tethered to the building.

"Well, Lawrence, I see you don't have a horse sergeant to keep the horses calm," Charlie said.

"No, my farmhand Daniel is doing the best he can," Lawrence said as he pointed in his direction. The horses were rearing up on their back legs, pulling at their reins, nipping at each other, and pushing him up against the barn with a crash.

"I think we better help you," Charlie said. All the soldiers got off their horses and went over to bring some semblance of order to the chaos of the mounts being ineptly handled by Daniel. The sound of their sabers rattling on their sides reminded Lawrence of the time he spent in the army.

"I see what's happening here," Sam Carpenter said. (He was the oldest soldier). He whispered to the horse nearest to the open door of the barn. "It's okay, fella." He stroked the horse and moved him down the line, closer to the farmhouse. "Let's get you away from that red, white, and blue paper snapping in the wind."

"Here, Sam," Eddie Johnson said. He dropped handfuls of hay and carrots at the hoofs of the horses. The hay rustled around their legs as they sniffed and snorted at the dried grass. "That did it." All at once, they calmed down and began to eat. Daniel backed away and let out a sigh of relief.

"We'll see you later, Lawrence," Sam said. "I've got your ring." He pointed to it in his pocket.

"Thanks, Sam," Lawrence said, and at the same time, patted him on the back as he and the rest of his army friends passed by on their way into the house. The touch of his shirt sent a surprising chill up Lawrence's spine.

Their boots clunked on the wooden porch when the soldiers went into the house, and their swords jingled against their sides as they went through the summer kitchen.

14

A MILITARY WEDDING

THE WEDDING WAS held in September on a Wednesday because the minister had a heavy schedule on the weekends. He was standing in the parlor at the bottom of the stairs, waiting for Abigail to come down; she was dressed in the typical Geneva gown. It consisted of a black robe, like a choir robe with bell-type sleeves and white tabs attached to the collar. He held tight to a little black Bible as he looked up toward the top of the landing.

Flowers were everywhere; under the handrails attached to the newels were large brightly colored, yellow flowers from the squash plant; orange blossoms lined the windows; ropes of smilax and little daisies ran around the pictures on the wall.

When Lawrence came into the sitting room, after greeting the guests, it was packed from wall to wall with people waiting to see the bride. He pushed his way through the swarm so that he was standing at the bottom of the set of steps. The smell and clouds of cigars and pipe smoke filled the room.

He longingly looked up at the top of the stairs like everybody else, expecting to see the seventeen-year-old farm girl transformed into a woman ready to get married.

Nobody was disappointed. Lawrence was awestruck. His eyes stayed riveted on her as she descended the staircase. It seemed to him as if she was floating over the flight of steps. She wore a pale-blue dress, all silk, satin, and lace supported by a cage crinoline. The veil on her head trailed to the back and was supported by a tiara made of real flowers.

Abigail had inherited her father's farmer mentality. She had told Lawrence, when he objected to a blue wedding dress instead of a white one, that nothing should go to waste and that she could possibly wear the dress for other occasions.

When she got to the bottom of the landing, she slipped her arm into Noah's arm in one motion. Then Noah walked her over to Lawrence, letting her go by putting her hand in Lawrence's hand. "Take care of her," he said.

The people parted to let them through. After crossing the living room, they stood motionless in front of the minister, waiting to be joined together as man and wife. They turned to each other and smiled. Lawrence leaned on his good right leg, tipping closer to Abigail and pressing against her crinoline cage frame that held up her dress.

In his mind's eye, he could see Burton's body in a heap on the rug. He was standing on the very spot where he was shot, although now it was clean of the blood. He scooted over and pulled Abigail with him so that he wasn't trampling on the man's grave.

The couple faced the minister. Lawrence noticed that the preacher bobbed and weaved, and the familiar smell of alcohol hung like a pungent cloud around him. Sam Carpenter stood shoulder to shoulder next to Lawrence, holding his hands behind himself as if he was at parade rest, waiting to be asked for the ring.

As the preacher got closer to the couple, Lawrence raised his eyebrows and thought, *Wow, I could get drunk just standing next to this guy.* The minister leaned closer into the couple. "Wilt thou have this woman to thy wedded wife, to live together after God's ordinance, in the holy state of matrimony? Wilt thou love her, comfort her, honor, and keep her, in sickness and health; and forsaking all others, keep thee only unto her, as long as ye both shall live?"

Lawrence said, "I will."

Then the minister asked Abigail the same questions when it came to Lawrence, and she said, "I will."

"Lawrence, take her right hand," the minister asked. "Say after me."

Lawrence repeated the words said by the minister. "I, Lawrence Ellsworth, take thee Abigail Wilson to be my wedded wife, to have and to hold, from this day forward, for better, for worse, for richer, for poorer, in sickness and in health, to love, and to cherish, till death do us part, according to God's holy ordinance, and thereto I plight thee my faith."

Then Abigail took Lawrence's right hand and said the same thing. "I, Abigail Wilson,…" Just as Abigail finished her vows, Lawrence's hand slipped out of hers.

Suddenly, Lawrence fainted and Sam caught him before he hit the floor. "What's up, Lawrence," Sam asked.

"I can't breathe. There's too many people in this parlor. They're sucking out all the air," Lawrence said.

"Take a couple of deep breaths. I'll hold you up," Sam said. He held Lawrence up, supporting him under his arms.

"Thanks." After a while, Lawrence stood up straight and took in a deep breath. Sam passed the ring to him, and he put it on Abigail's finger.

Then they turned and faced the guests. The arch of sabers immediately followed their ceremony. The saber bearers got into position, and then the senior sword bearer issued a queue, and all the sword bearers turned and proceeded into the middle of the sitting room.

The command of "center face" was given. They pivoted so that they were in two lines facing each other. "At the arch sabers" command was heard, and all at once, the sabers were raised in their right hands until the tips of all the swords were touching the tip of the sword directly opposite. The cutting edges were up.

After Lawrence and Abigail walked through the arch, the command "carry sabers" was given and then "rear face, forward march."

At the same time, as Abigail turned toward the doorway, one of the soldiers tapped her on the back of her dress with the flat part of the saber, and said, "Welcome to the army, miss."

She smiled and then moved toward the kitchen.

Lawrence turned all of a sudden into the room and said, "A reception will be held in the barn. All are welcome."

15

AN UNINVITED GUEST

BY NOW IT was noon time, and the sun was peeking through the oak trees on the southern side of the farmhouse. Abigail was negotiating her way through the parlor into the kitchen and eventually outside. She came to the kitchen entrance, turning sideways to squeeze her crinoline cage for her dress through the narrow door. She popped through the exit and finally stood on the porch. Lawrence followed right behind her. Then arm in arm, they strolled to the barn which had been decorated for the occasion.

The outside of the barn had a white curtain draped over the sliding door of the barn, and a long table was set up outside with straight-backed chairs and a white linen tablecloth draped over it for any people who wanted to eat outside.

Lawrence was captivated by the idea of decorating the dirty old barn into the beautiful venue for the reception. He remembered the barn when it had horses in the stalls and cows giving birth in the hay. He was proud of the transformation that he, Noah, and Daniel worked so hard to make it happen.

On the way to the barn, the couple saw a group of boys playing mumblety-peg in the dirt next to the table outside, flipping the pocketknife as close to their feet as possible. Lawrence laughed when he saw the boy who, without a doubt, had lost, trying to pull the knife out of the ground with his teeth. He remembered many times as a boy trying to pull the knife out of the ground. He felt his teeth ache from the thought of it.

They walked through the door of the barn. "Oh, Lawrence, it's beautiful," Abigail said.

The ceiling was high with exposed wooden beams; it was as if they were the wooden bones that held the barn together. He wondered if anybody saw the barn like he did and whether it was his illness that made him see it that way. He imagined himself in the bottom of the belly of a large wooden horse, the Trojan horse, like the one that the Greeks built, and that he was one of those elite forces of men that came out of the belly of the horse and won the war.

Every timber was wrapped with strings of flowers in accordance with an English architect that Lawrence had read about, Crevasse Wheeler; purple long stem flowers next to white petal magnolias, large petal yellow sunflowers next to pink zinnia's. The architect saw the world in shades of harmony and contrast, and that was the way they arranged the flowers, trying for contrast and harmony.

He remembered stringing the flowers together while Daniel climbed the pillars of the barn, tying them to every bare space that he could find. The dirty old barn was changed into a slice of heaven. The sun shot rays of light into the barn, and they danced off the dust floating in the air.

Just inside of the door was a blackboard set up on the floor and it had the message "Please find your table #" written on it. Next to it were tags hanging from a string suspended between two step ladders. "Should we take a tag, Lawrence?" Abigail asked. She reached up but stopped when Lawrence pulled her arm back.

"No, Abby, we sit at the head table. We're the guests of honor remember," he said with a smile.

"Oh yes, you're right." After that they walked into the barn.

Lawrence's army buddies were completely relaxed. Their blue jackets were slung over their chairs with their leather belts on top of their jackets. Everybody had their forage caps sitting on the table in front of them and their swords on a chair at the head of the table.

Every person clapped and two of his war buddies, Oliver Flood and Charlie Jillson, gave a "Hurrah, Hurrah, and *Rrrrr*," like a tiger growl and threw their hats in the air.

Abigail and Lawrence took their seats at a head table; one chair was labeled Groom and the other Bride. The table was set up deep in the back of the barn so that the couple could easily see everybody that came and went.

Sam Carpenter suddenly got up from his seat. While he was walking over to the table that was set up with the food, he said, "We're starving. We thought you'd never get here to the barn." The other soldiers followed him, and they all picked up dishes and went over to the tables filled with food. They all followed behind Sam. As he went by the table, he speared pieces of sirloin, hashed chicken, some stewed veal, and broke off some of the meat off a leg of mutton.

Charlie Jillson had trouble picking up the food and putting it in his plate with just one arm, so Eddie took two plates and slid them across the table as he put food in both of them. "I think that suckling pig is making eyes at me," Eddie said. They all laughed and then moved on, filling their glasses to the top with brandy. "Hey, what about that wedding cake. I sure would like to have a piece of that." A three-tiered white wedding cake sat in the middle of the table with tarts and confections surrounding it.

Although it was before they formally were to cut the cake to give to the guests, Lawrence turned to Abigail. "Is it all right for my men to cut a piece now," he asked. She nodded. Lawrence hollered across the barn, "Go ahead cut yourselves a piece but slice it from the top tier," he said.

They devoured the top section so the cake looked like an unfinished pyramid.

Oliver Flood walked over to the section of the table that had seafood on it. He picked up a red lobster and put it in the middle of his dish, and then he reached over and dropped clams and oysters around the lobster. They sounded like rocks plopping onto his plate. "Boy, these look good," he said. Then he scooped pieces of apple pie, pumpkin pie, and bread pudding onto the top of all the seafood.

All of a sudden, the band, consisting of a banjo, fiddle, and harmonica, started to play music like "Home Sweet Home" and "When This Cruel War Is Over," but they were tunes that were depressing and brought back sad memories to the soldiers, especially Lawrence. He thought about the band—a band that he had seen when he was in the army—that had a flute, a harmonica, and fiddle that was playing one minute next to his tent and then they were gone, blown up by a shell that had landed in the middle of them. It was so quick that all that was left were the echo of the music, their instruments, and their frosty breaths.

All of a sudden, Sam Carpenter shouted to the band, "Let's have a cotillion."

People got up and started to dance to "Yankee Doodle Dandy" and later "Tramp, Tramp, Tramp." They whirled and twirled around the barn, laughing and bumping into each other.

"Oh, Lawrence, will you dance with me?" Abigail asked.

"I'll try." He got up and took her by the hand and walked onto the dance floor. They started in stages at first then picked up speed to keep up with the rest of their guests. However, Lawrence kept tripping on Abigail's dress and apologizing every time he stumbled.

"It's all right, Lawrence," Abigail said. "I'll go in the house and get my walking dress on. It'll be easier to dance."

"Are you sure it's the right thing to do on your wedding?" he asked.

"It's my wedding, isn't it?" she asked. "Let people talk. I don't care. I want to dance."

She raced into the house and left Lawrence standing alone in the middle of the dancefloor while dancing couples twirled around him.

Charlie Jillson walked up to him. "What's going on, buddy?" he asked.

"She went into the house to change her dress." He looked calm and thoughtful at the barn door.

Charlie put his good right arm around Lawrence's shoulders. "Come on, let's get a beer."

They sat at the head table drinking their beers while the music got quicker and louder, and the dancers got more excited. "Does the place where they took off your arm bother you?" Lawrence asked.

"No, not really," he said. "But If I tell you something, you won't think I'm as crazy as a loon will you?" Charlie asked, leaning closer to Lawrence.

"No."

"Well, sometimes I get a lot of pain in an arm that's not even there anymore," he whispered.

Lawrence frowned and looked into the foam on the head of his beer. He wanted to tell Charlie about what phantoms were plaguing him, but instead he said, "We all have baggage that we brought back from the war. You're not crazy, Charlie."

Just as Lawrence tipped the mug up to his mouth to finish off what was left in the bottom of the glass, Abigail appeared.

"I'm ready," she said. Then she whirled around like a skater on the ice.

"Charlie, would you dance with Abigail?" Lawrence asked, moaning a bit because he lifted his leg and placed it in a more comfortable position under the table.

"Sure," he said. "You don't mind, do you, Abby?"

"No, not at all," she said, followed by her giggling with excitement.

Charlie got up and grabbed her hand, pulling her out on to the dancefloor. He spun Abigail around with his good arm held high in the air and then held her around the waist while they danced to the center of the floor. When they heard the do-si-do, they circled each other back to back. The band played a host of snappy songs: "Was My Brother in the Battle?," "Marching through Georgia," "When Johnny Comes Marching Home." They danced for an hour.

Lawrence was glad that Charlie was at the reception so that Abigail could enjoy dancing. If it were anybody else, Lawrence would have felt inadequate and jealous, but he respected Charlie and trusted him with his new bride. Besides, he thought, as he poured more beer into his glass, he lost his arm. He's in worse shape than me. He toasted them with his glass when they whooshed by and after that drank down a mouthful of beer.

He started to feel dizzy, and he knew that he was getting drunk. I can't dance, but at least this is something I can do well. *Get drunk*, he thought. Then he tipped the mug up to his mouth and drained the glass. "Ah, that was good," he said.

Everybody was having a great time. It was a scene of a happy bedlam. His soldier buddies were up and dancing with every girl they could find. Even the little children clumsily spun each other around the wooden dancefloor, possibly pretending they were somebody's parents. They laughed and ran back and forth between the grown-ups.

Running between the dancers were two scrawny bloodhound dogs barking and yelping. They chased after one another one minute and then, having their attention snatched away by a running child, went in that direction. But most of all, Lawrence noticed Abigail's face beaming with excitement. All the chaos behind and around Abigail faded away as if all the people were just background in a painting, and the only smiling happy face Lawrence could see was hers. She held Charlie with a light touch on his left side so as not to brush up against his amputated arm.

But all of a sudden, when the band stopped, everything became quiet again, and the blurred background of the dancefloor came into focus. John Webb stood in the open barn door with two of his soldiers on each side of him. They walked unhurried toward Lawrence who was sitting at the head table.

John walked up close to the table. "What, no invitation?" John Webb said. "I'll tell you what. You can cut the tally in half. It's my wedding present." He stood there looking around at the festive decorations. "You're having quite a party."

"You're right. Nobody invited you," Lawrence said. "So get out and leave me in peace on my wedding day." Lawrence realized that somehow John Webb had gotten in his head and knew the best ways to get at his most unprotected fears. He considered him a devil. And with this in mind, he recognized that John took pleasure in motiveless hatred and a strong desire to do harm. *The only way to combat him is to wait when he is most vulnerable and alone*, he thought.

"Now is that any way to treat a guest," John said. Then he pulled up a chair at the head table, poured himself a beer, and leaned back to enjoy the view. On both sides of him, his two companions both grabbed a bottle of beer, put their feet up on the white linen tablecloth, and gulped down their drinks. The two soldiers were covered with trail dust, and it billowed into the air when they plopped their boots on the clean white table.

Lawrence looked over at John. "What you're doing to me and this farm is wrong," Lawrence said.

"I don't care if you think it's right or wrong," John said. "I'm completely unconcerned with if you survive or pass on. The only things that are important to me are my prosperity and the care of my men. Everything else is insignificant."

By this time, Abigail and Charlie danced back to the table. "Well, that was fun," Charlie said. Then he sat down and tossed his soft felt hat on the table at the same time that he sat in the chair.

"Yes, I enjoyed it kind, sir," Abigail said. She curtseyed to him.

John Webb interjected. "So are you going to introduce me to this lovely young lady?" He turned to Lawrence and then looked back at Abigail and winked at her.

"This is Abigail Wilson," Lawrence said.

"No, Lawrence, Abigail Ellsworth. Remember."

"Oh, I'm sorry, Abby. My wife Abigail Ellsworth." Lawrence motioned toward Abigail with an open palm. Lawrence blushed with embarrassment at his stupid mistake.

"May I have the pleasure of this dance, Ms. Ellsworth?" John asked.

Lawrence was enraged by John's bad-mannered request. He got up at once and faced John. The instant he did that,

John's bodyguards stood up at the ready. "She's not dancing with you now or ever," Lawrence shouted.

"Lawrence, don't be so rude to our guest. Of course, I'll dance with you," Abigail said.

"Thank you, kind miss. You do a soldier a great kindness," John said. He grabbed her and twirled out onto the dancefloor.

16

A Naive Girl

"What's your name, sir? My husband neglected to tell me when we were introduced," she said.

They twirled and moved rhythmically in time to the music. Abigail smiled, reveling in the feel of her body being as light as a feather. Her heart tickled her belly as she floated over the dancefloor. She had been dancing for over an hour, but for some reason, she didn't feel tired and still wanted to dance the rest of the night away.

"My name is John Webb, miss. It seems as if your husband had a little bit too much to drink."

"Yes, I think you're right," she said with a frown on her brow.

"You already know my name, but what you don't know is that I originally came from Kentucky. I guess you'd call me a Southern gentleman."

"You're a reb?" She stopped dancing all at once with her nose turned up. She stood still with her arms folded across her chest. "You're an enemy. What are you doing here?"

"I fought for the Union. My family was Southerners. My loyalties go to whoever is on the winning side." He tried to pull her arm away so they could start dancing again, but she stood fast not budging. In a final desperate move, he bowed down in front of her and dipped his hat in a big arc and looked up. "Even though I'm a reb which you hate, I'm still a gentleman that would love to dance with you. Be my princess and I'll be your knight."

Her young farm girl heart melted when she heard John's words. All her ideas about the glorious noble war came true when John bowed to her. She uncrossed her arms and walked over to him like a queen, holding her hand out. "You may take my hand, knight," she said. A delightful surge of excitement ran up her spine.

He snatched her away onto the dancefloor, and as they twirled to the music holding tight to each other, they stole tidbits of information about each other's lives. "If it makes you feel any better, my family washed their hands of me when I joined the Union. I not only lost a family, but they cut me out of any inheritance that I was going to get. They were very rich." Because Abigail was captivated by what John was talking about, she listened most of the time.

Meanwhile, Abigail noticed that Lawrence was getting more and more agitated. "We better go back to the table. My husband is getting up and is coming over here," she said.

The couple walked back to the head table with Abigail pulling up the rear as any young woman of the time would do. Again, before Abigail sat down, John bowed and took off his hat to show respect. "I salute you, madam," he said.

Lawrence grabbed John Webb by the collar. "Stay away from my wife," he said.

The two soldiers sitting at the table who came with John got up all of a sudden and started to approach Lawrence. They had their hands on their pistols as they come within reach of him. At the same time, Charlie got up and drew his pistol out of his holster. From across the barn getting nearer were Oliver Flood, Sam Carpenter, and Eddie Jillson. Their boots clunked on the wooden flooring, their sabers rattled by their sides, and Eddie spit a mouthful of tobacco on the floor just before he got up to run to Lawrence's rescue.

They reached the head table and the two opposing sides crashed into each other. Lawrence shoved Abigail aside. "I don't want you involved in this, Abby," he said and then kissed her on the cheek. There was a clatter of overturned chairs, the sound of shattering plates, and the metal "shing" sound of the sabers being pulled from their scabbards.

Abigail rubbed her sore wrist where Lawrence had grabbed her. She backed into a chair and overturned it, trying to get away from the skirmish. When she looked at her wrist, she wondered whose droplets of sweat those were that were pooling on top of her hands. She came to the conclusion that they were Lawrence's, and they came from his sweaty palms. The smell of stale beer and the rancid odor of nervous sweat formed a fog over the fighting men.

Being a child of the farm, she only knew the birth, death, and struggle of the plants and animals that lived in Noah Wilson's world. *Men are strange beasts*, Abigail thought. They consume us like food and then leave us alone and only come back when they are hungry again. But more than that was the fact that she was overwhelmed by all the attention that she was receiving. John was only the second man whom she knew that had been away to distant lands and seen foreign people.

The heroes that she read about were coming true, and she wanted to hold on to that excitement for as long as she could.

The guests on the other side of the barn turned into a mass of swelling and heaving humanity. They became a bloated serpent hypnotized by the battle going on at the back of the barn. Children hid behind their mother's skirts, young couples hugged each other for comfort, and older men were being pulled back by their wives because those aging soldiers wanted to get into the fight.

Abigail's heart was divided. She loved Lawrence, but she also wanted to hear more about the chivalrous days of the war from John. *He described the war just like I imagined it*, she thought.

All the soldiers that were Lawrence's friends pointed their swords at John and his two bodyguards. The two soldiers still had their guns in their holsters because

Lawrence's friends pounced on them, holding their swords to their throats.

"I'm not going to tell you again," Lawrence said. "I don't want to have anything to do with you from now on."

By this time, Noah had come over to see what all the commotion was about.

"Hi, Abby, Lawrence," Noah said. "What's goin' on?"

"We had a little disagreement, Pa. That's all. Yeah, a little disagreement, that's all it was," Lawrence said. Abby saw that Lawrence was upset, but it seemed to her that he wanted to get rid of John in a big hurry. *It's because he's jealous*, she thought. Even though she saw his eyes staring at John and his nostrils flared which told her that he was angry, she still thought that he was lying about the reason because he leaned away from Noah, slightly shrugging his shoulders and lowering his head.

Noah stared at John Webb. "Didn't I throw you off my land a while back?" Noah asked.

"Yes, sir, you did," John said.

"Then what are ya' doin' back here?"

"Pa, let's just kick him out of here," Lawrence said. "He wasn't even invited."

"Hold up, Lawrence," Noah said.

"I'm here because your son-in-law owes me," John said.

"Owes you? What does he mean?" Noah turned to Lawrence.

"He was blackmailing me." He sat heavily on the table behind him in an abrupt manner. "He demanded a tally of produce every week or else he was going to take Daniel away and poison our well."

"Put your swords up, men," Noah said. "These soldiers will leave peacefully, won't you?"

John looked timid now. "Let's go, boys." They looked defeated as they left the barn. John glanced at Abigail as he left.

She couldn't help it, but she felt an approving smile form on her lips in spite of all that had just taken place, and the fact that he was without a doubt an opportunist and evil. She was drawn to him like a moth to a flame. She knew she was going to get burned, but she just couldn't help herself.

"By the way, third time is the trick," Noah said. "If I see you, I'll kill you on sight the next time."

By now, the commotion had settled down, and most of the guests continued eating and drinking, dancing, and laughing. The meal went on until twilight. Some of the guests got up and walked out of the barn to walk off some of the meal and to relax. Some of the guests fell asleep in the chairs and still others went outside to attend to the horses. There were guests who left as soon as the sun went down, herding their children into the carriages so that they could put them to bed.

Abigail felt sad to see people leaving, but she realized that they had their own lives, and that her wedding couldn't go on forever, although she wanted it to. Outside the barn, there was the clatter of people getting into their carriages and the jingle of the harnesses being put on their horses along with muffled speech.

But what made her happy were the people who stayed behind and spent the night in the summer kitchen drinking rum, smoking, laughing, and talking about how nice the wedding was.

Although what pleased her the most was the fact that people set up tents on the lawn next to the pump and stayed all night and into the next day. Lawrence's army buddies set up their little white, what were called, dog tents all in a row next to each other. They spent the night around the fire smoking, drinking, and reminiscing about their time in the army.

Having all these different people around was more excitement than she had ever had in her whole life. There were more people on the farm than she had ever seen. She wanted it to last forever.

17

THE TRIP TO NEW YORK

AT THE CRACK of dawn the next morning, Abigail and Lawrence walked out the front door of the house and into the fields next to the pump. Lawrence saw everything this morning as fresh, new, and brimming with promise. He had his arm around her waist, and as they walked, he kissed her on the lips and on the neck from time to time. It felt so right having her next to him. He imagined that having Abigail as his wife was like Charlie feeling an arm that was no longer there, but knowing that there was supposed to be something there to complete him. *She was that arm that was missing in my life, and she was here on the farm all the time right in front of me*, he thought.

They walked up to Lawrence's buddies. Even though the war was over, the men were still in the habit of setting up their camp as if at any minute they would be ordered to saddle up and attack the enemy. A fire was still burning when they approached the four white dog tents. Their rifles were next to the fire, leaning up against each other in a pyramid shape. On each shelter, a canteen and a tin cup hung on the stick that held up the tent and a knapsack was at the opening.

"Hey, you fresh fish, get up and greet the day," Lawrence shouted. Then he went over to each tent, grabbing a hold of it and shaking it. Abigail could be heard in the background laughing.

"Gee, are they still alive?" Abigail asked.

"Oh yeah. They're just pickled," Lawrence snickered under his breath.

Sam Carpenter lifted his forage cap off his face and looked up at Lawrence. "What the hell is going on?" he said.

Lawrence looked back at Abigail realizing that she wasn't used to hearing such foul language. "Watch what you say, Sam, my wife is here."

"Oh, I didn't realize it was you. I got a little bit corned last night. Sorry," he said as he slid himself out from on top of his rubber ground sheet. It made a crackling sound when he finally managed to stand up in front of the tent.

"That's okay, but my wife is my new recruit. She's not used to hearing that kind of language," Lawrence said.

Sam looked up at Abigail and smiled. "I'll watch it from now on."

"Make some coffee, Sam," Lawrence said.

"At least your front yard isn't like travelin' with the Burnside campaign," he said. "There was so much mud there that we had to be dug out of bed."

The coffeepot and the cups dinged in the early morning after Sam whipped out the dew that had pooled in the bottom of the cups while he made the coffee.

Then he and Abigail sat on two stumps gazing into the fire. Lawrence laughed at the little poem and was supremely content until Sam brought up the subject of Burton. Sam turned to Abigail and asked her jokingly, "What kind of sergeant are you?" He scooped the coffee into the coffeepot while he looked over his shoulder at her. "Are you like that unfair, Sgt. Burton? He always gave his pets all the soft jobs. And when he was the orderly sergeant, he divided the rations unequally whenever they were spread out on that rubber blanket."

Lawrence's stomach clenched when he thought about Burton. "No, she's a good sergeant. And I follow her orders to the letter," he said.

Lawrence could see how Abigail was nervous at the mention of Burton's name. She became withdrawn and stared into the fire. "That's right, a good sergeant," she said.

"Oh, by the way, I thought you came back here with him. Where is he? He owes me money," Sam said.

"He, ah…he left," Lawrence stood up and bent over. He poured the coffee from the pot into his tin cup and then stared into the steaming coffee.

The ghost of Burton again disturbingly invaded their lives. The soldiers heard the conversation going on outside their dog tents, and one by one, they came out of their shelters like zombies, at a snail's pace, walking over to the coffeepot hanging on the hook suspended over the fire. They groaned and stretched and said hello before they sat with a thump on the remaining logs around the fire. Burton's spirit invaded the conversation.

"Boy, he was a mean one, that serge," Sam said.

"Yeah, he wouldn't let me have a chaw of tobacco until I worked out the difference between my right foot and my left," Eddie Johnson said.

"You were lucky. He smacked me with that willow stick that he carried with him every time I got off on the wrong foot when we marched. I guess it was because I was so young, and he wanted to teach me a lesson," Oliver Flood said. "Boy, I can still feel that stick on my legs and back."

"The thing that really got me about him was what he did with the prisoners we had in Alton prison. Most of the prisoners were dying of small pox anyway, but to take any gold or valuables from them besides starvin' them was a sin," Sam said.

"Well, we're all packed and ready to go to New York for our honeymoon," Lawrence said. It was a relief to change the subject.

As soon as Abigail got up, all of Lawrence's buddies went over to the couple and hugged Abigail and shook Lawrence's hand, wishing them a good trip and a happy marriage.

As they walked away, Lawrence could breathe again. And Abigail clung to him just like before. "It'll be fun, Abigail. Have you ever been to New York before?"

"No. I just read about it in a book," she said.

"You'll never forget it. I promise you."

It was eleven in the morning and Lawrence, with Daniel's help, loaded the heavy trunk in the rear of the carriage. Daniel rode in the back while Abigail and Lawrence were in front. Daniel was to take the carriage back to the farm after the couple boarded the boat *Continental*, which was a large paddle wheel steamboat.

When they got to New Haven, they would go on the craft that would take them to New York. All the departures were at 3:15 p.m. and 11:00 p.m. They were night voyages.

The two-seater four-passenger Banner Wagon with removable top and seats and a drop down tailgate had the couples trunk stored under the backseat.

"We have to leave now, Abigail," Lawrence said as he snapped the reins over the horse's rump. It was now a little after eleven o'clock, and there was a frost covering summer's face. The cold weather of September was creeping up from the ground and grabbing hold of the flowers and delicate plants of the forest. The icy breath of the season was hiding in every valley.

"Thank you for this cushion for me to sit on," Abigail said as she wiggled into the pillow with her rear end. Then leaned over and grabbed Lawrence's arm and nestled into his shoulder. A slight wisp of frost came from her mouth.

"It's okay, my darling. Nothing is too good for my bride," he said. "Besides, it's a good three- or four-hour ride to the steamboat." He then reached into his pocket and pulled out a crumpled-up piece of newspaper. "I found this description in an old daily that I found under the sink. Would you like to read it?"

"Yes." Abigail sat up right away and took the article from his hand. "I can't read it, Lawrence, the wagon is bouncing too hard."

He pulled the carriage over and then took it from her hand. "I'll read it to you, Abigail," he said. "Published April 27, 1865. The railroad and steamboat connection between the New-York and New-Haven steamboats, and the New-Haven, and Springfield Railroad commences May 1, the trains running to and from the steamboat wharf at New Haven. Nothing could better suit the convenience and comfort of travelers in that direction. The first-class steamers of this line leave New York daily at 3:15 and 11 p.m. (Sundays excluded)."

"That sounds so exciting, Lawrence. I've never been on the steamboat before," she said.

"I hear they're pretty luxurious." Lawrence heard Abigail giggle like a little girl, and it made him so happy that he felt like screaming into the sky. So he did. "Ahh!" he screamed.

They both laughed when Daniel woke up all of a sudden. "What...what's goin' on?" he shouted.

"It's okay, Danny. Go back to sleep," Lawrence said as he turned around to see that Daniel was all right and to reassure him.

After that, Lawrence snapped the reins over the horse's rump, and they were on the way.

The carriage continued to plod along, bouncing over the ruts in the road and kicking up the dust. Daniel fell asleep in the back of the carriage again while Abigail continued holding tight to Lawrence.

Lawrence could feel the excitement in his belly. For the longest time, phantoms of the war stood guard over his feelings of contentment. They were like sentinels preventing any true pleasure from passing by. But now with Abigail by his side and the expectation of the great honeymoon that he had planned in their future, he was feeling everything with an intensity he had never experienced before.

Being September, the New England trees started to turn colors. Vivid oranges, yellows, and reds were painted on the trees like an intense Van Gogh painting. As they rode in the carriage, he bent his neck down and kissed Abigail square on the lips. It tasted sweet as honey, and he thought that maybe her virgin kisses would make him pure again. He rubbed his lips on her cheek, and he imagined that it felt as soft as the fur on a newborn doe's belly. When she leaned up against him, his imagination conjured up the image of a white rabbit with a pink nose—innocent and fragile. This was the world that he wanted to be in.

He had come from a world of fear and loathing into what he understood as the normal world. Here, there were no bombs, there were no screams of men dying in agony, and there was no hunger. Everything now was as he expected it to be, and he wanted it to last forever.

He felt in control now, not only with his emotions, but physically holding the reins to the wagon, aware that he was in command of their direction. Any farm house or neighborhood that he recognized passed by as they got farther and farther away from the farm. The forest around them got thick with stands of white birch, pine, and oak. And the influence of man became less and less. They rode on a thin ribbon of road snaking its way south to New Haven.

After almost two hours of driving to their destination of New Haven and the boarding of the 280-foot paddle wheel steamboat *Continental*, Lawrence woke everybody up. "Wake up, everybody," he said. Abigail and Daniel both stretched and yawned.

"Are we there, Mista' Lawrence?" Daniel asked.

"No. I just want to rest and water the horse." Lawrence drove over a wooden bridge. The clatter of the wagon wheels and the clip-clop of the horse's metal horseshoes echoed in his ears.

"This is beautiful, Lawrence," Abigail said as she looked around.

Lawrence tied the horse to the branch of northern pine, and then Abigail and Daniel went down to the stream and sat where it narrowed to rush under the bridge.

But Lawrence walked to the nearby pond where tall brown cattails grew next to the shore, and those familiar dragonflies that greeted him as a boy darted between the plants and skimmed along the surface of the water. He snapped a cattail off and tossed it into the pool.

On each side of the brook, two drooping weeping willows let their slender green leaves hang down into the fast-moving stream. Abigail had her shoes off and was splashing her feet in the cool water when Lawrence approached through a forest of American beech trees and sugar maples.

"Great, isn't it, Abby?" Lawrence asked.

"I'm in heaven," she said and then arched her neck back to get a kiss from Lawrence.

Meanwhile, Daniel was attending to the horse.

"That piney smell from the trees reminds me of the grove of pine that we have back home," he said. Then he waded into the middle of the stream, cupped his hands, and took a long deep drink of the ice cold water. "But that mildew damp smell coming from under the bridge brings back bad memories."

"What do you mean, Lawrence?" she asked. By now, she had her hands in back of her, supporting her weight, staring at Lawrence with a frown on her face.

"Don't look at me like I'm crazy, Abby," he said. "When I was away at war, I was bending down one day in a stream, just like this one, to get a drink of water next to a small wooden bridge, just like this one. The only difference was that the water that I had been drinking was blood red, and

I hadn't noticed it. I waded through the brook and saw a dead Union soldier and a Reb stuck under the bridge, bleeding into the stream. If I look into this stream I can still see those two soldiers." Lawrence, all at once submerged his head into the fast-moving river and then just as quickly pulled his head out of the cold water. It tumbled off his hair in a long rivulet of crystal blue liquid. "Ahhh, that's better," he said, followed by him wiping his face and hair with his hands.

"I don't understand why these things happen to you all the time, Lawrence," Abigail said as she sat up. She folded her hands together and put them between her legs. She stared at Lawrence considerately waiting to hear the answer. She leaned forward as if she was going to hear the answer to the most profound question ever asked.

Seeing how intent she was, Lawrence wanted to give her an answer that would not only satisfy her, but also him. The moss-covered bank of the stream hung over the water. Lawrence walked over to Abigail and started to wash her bare feet that were suspended just above the surface of the stream. While washing her feet, he smiled at her and thought about her question, not paying very much attention to the pressure of the water gushing over his legs. "Do you know that you're the only one that ever asked me that question?"

"No, I didn't know that," Abigail said.

"Well, you are." Lawrence stopped rubbing her feet and then sat down beside her. "I have a lot of shortcomings and weaknesses, Abby. When I came back from the war, I was aware of what I could be or should be—someone more honest, more courageous. But the demons that I brought back with me from the war wouldn't let me do that."

"I wish I could help somehow, Lawrence," she said.

"I appreciate that and love you for it, but there's nothing you can do. I have to live with this sickness, I guess."

"But it seems as if it happens all at once."

"No, Abby, it's triggered by things that I see, sounds that I hear, smells that remind me of a time during the war. Even my buddies from the war that attended the wedding brought back bad memories. How could I explain to them what was happening to me? I couldn't."

"I think I understand now," Abigail said.

"And another curious thing is that some of the memories of the war which I should remember, I don't," he said. "When I saw all those men dead on the battlefield in the middle of the day, I should have remembered every detail but I don't. It's as if my mind couldn't accept what was happening. You could walk on the dead from one end of the field to the other without ever touching the ground with your feet. So my mind made me think it was a nightmare, and I didn't know if it really happened or not."

"That explains a lot," Abigail said.

"Before I came back from the war, I felt alone and abandoned by humanity. My emotions were flat because it hurt when I remembered. It felt better just to be numb.

The only things that preoccupied my mind were death. I was always watching and alert for a sniper behind a tree or a soldier with a saber in his hand ready to run me through. I couldn't tolerate any frustrating situation."

"Does it help that I'm listening?" she asked.

"Yes, it does help. I wish you could feel the weight that is lifted off my shoulders when I tell you about what happened during the war and how it has affected me," he said. "Now that you know better about what is happening to me, I think our marriage has a chance, otherwise, staying together would have been impossible."

"At least you're not arrogant, Lawrence, like in the *Iliad*, where the immortals punished those mortals who thought they were above the gods," she said.

"I don't think we have to worry about that, Abby. Let's not have all this ruin our honeymoon. Let's go!"

After all was said and done, Abby picked up her shoes, ran up the hill, and got back in the wagon. Daniel was already there, sleeping. Lawrence came up the hill, holding tight to the seat, he took off his boots and dumped out the water that had collected inside of them and then slipped them back on. A minute later, he sat next to Abigail, reached down and grabbed the reins, slapping them over the rump of the horse.

"Wake up, Daniel, we're off again," Abigail shouted.

While they rode to New Haven, Lawrence felt better for the moment, knowing that there was a bridge of understanding between him and Abigail. But he was still afraid for them, afraid for their ignorance of the future, and afraid of losing the emotions that Abigail stirred in him that had been buried.

She took away some of the numbness, some of the sadness, but just like in combat, you couldn't depend on what seemed to be evident. *Your position on the battlefield could change at any minute*, he thought.

"Prepare yourself, Abby, for things and people you never thought existed. For places you only dreamed of in fairytales," Lawrence said.

"I can't wait," she said. "Can't you just tell me a little bit about what's gonna happen?"

"You'll see."

"When I went into the army, we had a couple of days in New York. During that time, I went to the museum. And I was amazed at all the things in the world that I didn't know about."

18

A Strange
but Wonderful Trip

Abigail's back hurt and her rear end was sore from bouncing on the seat. After three hours of traveling, they started to see farmhouses and long white picket fences paralleling the road. While they rode by one of the fields, a chestnut stallion saw them and ran parallel to the fence. At the end of the fence appeared what seemed to be the owner of the property. He was dropping bales of hay off in the field; they were still green.

"Hello, neighbor," Lawrence said as he pulled up on the reins. "Whoa," he hollered. "I was wondering what the best road is to get to New Haven."

As she looked at the man, she thought to herself that he reminded her of Noah and that people seem the same no matter where you went. They worked hard; they loved their little piece of land. They were willing to help each other, and they wished only the best to every stranger.

The man jumped off his wagon and came over to the fence, putting his elbows on the top of it. He was dressed in overalls and had a yellow straw hat on his head. "Well, if you're going down toward the shore of New Haven, the left fork in the road would be the best. But if you're going into the center of town, the right fork would be the best," he said.

"Thank you, sir," Lawrence said. Then he slapped the reins over the rump of the horse and went down the left fork toward the wharfs. Abigail looked back, and the man had taken off his hat and was waving good-bye with it.

"I smell something, Lawrence," she said.

"Yeah, I smell it to. It's the sea, Abby."

They traveled down the left fork in the road until it went toward the shore. The road became easier to drive on, the closer they got to the city. All the ruts and holes were filled in so that the ride became more and more pleasant, and their excitement built with every mile.

Many of the houses on the way had anchors painted white on each side of their door as a decoration. And on many of the houses on the front gate, there were buoys painted with blue and red stripes. They were attached to large hemp ropes and hung down among intricate black nets.

"I don't see any plows or picks and shovels, just boats, anchors and ropes," Abigail said.

"I know, Abby, it seems were getting closer and closer to the ocean," Lawrence said. "They farm the sea like we farm the land."

As soon as Lawrence said that, the road turned into the entrance to a wooden dock. He pulled up on the reins, and they all sat there watching the hustle and bustle happening in front of them; two white horses attached to ropes and pulleys strained hard, lifting cargo out of the bottom of the boat next to the dock. Next to the laboring horses were two men, one wearing checkered pants and a close-fitting vest. The other man, dressed in a heavy jacket and bowler hat, was pulling and balancing a handcart with four wooden casks, while the man with the checkered pants pushed from behind.

Everywhere one looked, you could see men with cargo on their shoulders. And next to the clipper ships, wagons full of produce and freight were being lowered down onto the dock.

"Look at those large sailboats, Lawrence," Abigail said. "The rigging and the ropes look like spiderwebs, and the masts reach up to the sky. There's men in the rigging hanging off of the ropes."

Sandwiched between all the large sailing ships was the *Continental*, one of the largest side-wheeled paddleboats that went to New York. It sat there in the still waters of the wharf waiting for its passengers. It's two tall black stacks billowed gray smoke into the sky. "Look, Abby, that's the boat we're going on to go to New York," Lawrence said. "It's over two-hundred-eighty feet long."

"It looks like a fire breathing dragon, Lawrence," she said as she stared at the boat. "And it sounds like it's going to fall apart."

"I think that's just the sound of the boiler and the rattle of the paddle wheels. Don't be afraid of its roar, Abby, it won't bite you."

Daniel leaned forward. "Don't be afraid, Miss Abby. It looks scarier than it really is," he said. "I never been on the steamboat before, but I reckon it's just the same as being on a sailboat, just a little noisier."

Abigail turned around and patted Daniel's hand. "Thank you, Daniel. That was kind of you to try to make me feel better."

"My pleasure, miss," he said.

Lawrence snapped the reins over the rump of the horse, directing him toward the engine-powered boat. They had stopped many times to avoid the freight that was being pulled out of the holds of vessels as they swung over and dropped it on the docks. After dodging the freight coming off the large clippers, they were finally in front of the steamship.

Daniel and Lawrence went to the back of the carriage and lifted out a little butternut patina hand trunk and then picked up the larger flat top, dark red, mahogany steam trunk along with three carpetbags. They all sat on the dock, anxiously waiting to be picked up by one of the porters.

Two porters came down the gangplank and walked over to Lawrence. He gave them their tickets, and they grabbed the bags and brought them up to the steamer, putting them in their cabin.

"Thanks, Daniel," Lawrence said. He shook his hand, and as he did, he said, "Come back tomorrow and we'll be ready to go back to the farm. I don't know, I guess about the same time. Wait at the telegraph office, and I'll send you a message."

The couple waved good-bye as Daniel, at a snail's pace, negotiated his way through all the commotion of everyone coming and going on the wharf.

"Well, let's get on the ship," Lawrence said. They walked up along a narrow gangplank near the front of the ship. The craft had long narrow deck houses running the length of the vessel, which were the first class passenger's deck cabins. One of these cabins was reserved for Lawrence and Abigail. It would be their honeymoon suite.

The couple walked down into a long spacious eating area used as a recreation room for writing, reading, talking, and drinking when meals were not being served. There were two long tables that ran the length of the place.

"This is great, Lawrence. Is this where we'll eat?" she asked. She ran her hands over the lace tablecloths. They felt smooth to the touch.

"No, Abby. We have our own cabin. After all, we are royalty," Lawrence said. "We can eat in our cabin if we want to."

They both laughed and comically put their noses up to the ceiling while they strutted, pretending to be above it all.

"Oh, let's go see what it looks like," she said as she pulled at Lawrence's arm. "Where is it anyway?" she asked.

"Down the stairs to the right," Lawrence said, pointing to the door at the end of the hall.

She pulled at Lawrence's arm so that he had to hop to keep up with her. "Come on. Come on, I want to see what it looks like."

"Right there, Abby," he said as he pointed to the door on his right.

The narrow hallway smelled as if it had just been painted as the walls were stained with a cherry tint. Abigail threw open the door. Then she ran through the room and jumped on the brass bed. The springs squeaked, and she could smell the fresh clean odor of just washed sheets and pillowcases.

Washing the linens for the beds was a chore that she did many times at home but here it was done for her. Anyone else would've said that it was a small thing, but to her it was like being given a gift at Christmas that you waited for the whole year long. She buried her face in the fresh smelling pillow and took a deep breath.

"Isn't it grand Lawrence?" She asked.

"Are you happy Abby?"

"Oh yes, very."

"Come here Abby," Lawrence said. She got up and went over to the door where Lawrence was standing. He picked her up in his arms. "I have to carry you over the threshold." His perspiration made her head swim. It smelled like every great aroma that she had ever known; the smell of new mown hay, the smell of just cooked apple pie, the smell of turkey on Thanksgiving. She thought the only way she could understand these scents was to tell herself that they made her feel safe and at home.

But it did more to her than just that. It made her feel like a young woman—a young woman ready to give herself to her young man. She grabbed his arms and pulled them closer to her. "Let's make love, Lawrence," she said. His arms wrapped her in a cocoon of passion.

He carried her over to the bed and placed her gently on it. Then he lay next to her. This time, when they made love, it was not awkward or tentative, it was slow, methodical, and tender. This time, they had truly become man and wife. After a while, they both fell asleep and when Lawrence woke up, the ship was already on its way to New York.

19

BARNUM'S WORLD

LAWRENCE SAT UP and with care, like a ghost, slid off the bed. He was careful not to wake Abigail. He looked out the porthole and saw the lights of buildings on the shore reflected off the ocean. They were underway, and he had no idea just how long that was.

He walked out of the room and then went up on the deck. His foot felt good, now that he had just got out of bed. Lawrence left his cane in the corner of the room. He walked by a sailor with a coil of rope over his shoulder. He was dressed in the typical navy uniform with an open-collared jumper, a flat hat, and a flared pair of loose pants. "What time you got, sailor?" Lawrence asked.

The sailor reached into his pocket and pulled out a gold-plated pocket watch and opened it up. "Six thirty or thereabouts," he said.

"When do you think that we'll pull into New York?" Lawrence asked.

"We're coming up to the harbor right now," the sailor said, pointing toward the shore.

"Good. We're going to see the new *P.T. Barnum Show*."

"You got plenty of time, buddy. We should be pulling into the dock any minute now," the sailor said. "I saw that show. It's unbelievable. There's things he's got that will make you doubt your sanity. And I've been all over the world and seen just about everything."

"Yeah, I know a lot about doubting your sanity," Lawrence said. It was dusk by now, and there was a glow in the sky above the city. "What is that glow, sailor?" When Lawrence went into the army, he rode on a large clipper ship, and it was during the day. He had never seen the city at night.

"Why, those are all the gas lights of the city," he said.

"Abby has just got to see this," Lawrence said. He turned quickly and hobbled back toward the cabin. This was what he lived for, sharing the wonders of the world with Abigail. He hoped his excitement would be contagious. Lawrence moved over to Abigail and talked softly to her. "Abby, Abby, wake up. There's something you got to see." He shook her gently.

"What's the matter, are we sinking?" She reached up and grabbed a lifebelt that was slung in a shelf above the bedhead. She started to put her arm in the life preserver.

"No. You've just got to see this."

Abigail slid her feet off the bed and onto the floor. She sat there for a while, trying to wake up. She left the life jacket on the bed and walked over to the cherry wood washstand. After pouring the water into the large wash basin, she splashed her face with water. "Ahh, that's better," she said.

Lawrence grabbed her hand and pulled her out the door and then up on deck. It was like when they first met when they were children. He was showing her the way again; only now, they knew each other, and now everything seemed twice as good.

"Look," he said. "Look at all those lights. Have you ever seen so many lights in your whole life?"

"No. It turns the night into day. If we had those kinds of lights on the farm, we could harvest twenty-four hours a day," she said. She held tight to the railing and Lawrence stood behind her. He smelled the salt of the sea and felt the curve of Abigail's back against his stomach.

"We're pulling into the dock," Lawrence said, and at the same time, pointed toward the shore.

The ship slowed its motors so that it drifted toward the wharfs. When they got close enough, the engines were turned off, and men on the starboard side threw large hemp ropes to sailors already on the dock. The ropes clunked on the dock and the men picked them up in a hurry and draped them over the wood pilings.

The gangplank was lowered with a clang; the porters brought their baggage down to the wharf and put the trunks and bags in a cab. The couple rushed to the hotel to drop off their bags because there was a show in the new American Museum that Lawrence planned to see.

Abigail ran down the stairs of the hotel, but Lawrence skipped on the flight of steps, grabbing onto the rail trying to keep up and putting his cane under his arm. He wanted desperately to make it seem as if he could do anything Abigail could do in spite of his leg. Then when they were out on the sidewalk, Lawrence pointed to the bus with his cane. "That's the one we have to take," he shouted.

"Wait, Abigail, let's go into this jewelry store," Lawrence shouted. "There's plenty of buses that go by that way. We'll catch another one."

"Okay," Abigail said as she walked back to Lawrence's side.

"Let's go in here. There looks like there's some interesting things in this jewelry store." On the sidewalk, there were two gas lamps that illuminated the store. The light penetrated the large glass window revealing necklaces, broaches, and earrings made out of gold and silver.

When they got inside, there were all kinds of rings and costume jewelry being displayed on the counters. Without any hesitation, Abigail walked over to a snake necklace with realistic gold scales and turquoise. It was a necklace that was worn close to the neck. "Oh, Lawrence, I love this," she whispered to him as she cradled it in her hands.

"If you like it, then it's yours," Lawrence said. "And what about these Florentine earrings, would you like them too? They have flowers on them, and the edging is gold to match your necklace."

"Oh yes. I feel like I'm all possessed by the devil. I'm so excited."

"I understand, Abby. Just be happy, they're all yours," Lawrence said. "Now you can be highfalutin, just like all those ladies you see with their diamonds and pearls. I'll have to bow to you and kiss your hand every time we meet."

"No, you don't have to do that, Lawrence. Just treat me nice. That's all I want."

Lawrence paid the man standing behind the counter. He had on a bowler hat, tight-fitting vest, and an eye loop over his wire-rimmed glasses. "Thank you, sir," he said. Then he turned to Abigail. "Enjoy your new jewelry, miss."

They left the store and went out to the sidewalk to wait for another means of transportation. Abigail ran ahead to catch another omnibus that went to the museum. Lawrence was happy to see that she stopped the bus. When she got onto it, she turned to the driver and shouted, "Stop, Mister, my husband is coming." Lawrence hobbled up to the bus, grabbing the steel pole and then throwing his cane to Abigail. After that, he lifted himself into the vehicle.

They both laughed, trying to catch their breath as they finally were able to relax, knowing that they were safe on the omnibus. They went up the stairway in the front and sat down quickly in seats on the top floor. Abigail kept feeling her necklace and pinching her ears to make sure that she didn't lose her precious jewelry.

The bedlam of the city was deafening, and all of Lawrence's senses were alive; a faint smell of popcorn, cooked meat, and roasted coffee, baking bread, the sound of horses clopping on the cobblestones, carriages rumbling their wheels, people howling across the streets, policeman with their billy clubs thumping criminals over the head, a band blaring their horns into the air and banging on their drums on the corner of the street, the vibration of the bus on his back and legs, Abigail's tight grip in the palm of his hand. The voice of the city screamed in their ears.

"Where are we going?" Abigail asked.

"The museum is on Broadway between Spring and Prince Streets. We should be there any minute," he said. He had to shout to her, even though she was sitting right next to him. He chuckled inside, thinking how different it was from the silence of the farm. *Maybe that's why people came to the city. They didn't want to listen to the silence in their heads*, he thought.

As they got closer to the museum, people were walking on the sidewalks dressed in their finest. The men had tall top hats on, and many of them carried ornate gold top canes. The women's hats were large, brimmed, and colorful. The women's bustles seemed, to him, to stick out a little bit farther than he had remembered. There were people already in line waiting to get in.

The double deck omnibus pulled up in front of the three-story granite building. The bus was gaily colored—red, pink, and blue—with flowers and coaching scenes painted on the side. On the front of the building was the words Barnum's American Museum. Lawrence and Abigail walked down the stairs and up to the front door because by now the line had thinned out and most people were in the building. Lawrence put sixty cents into the hand of an usher dressed in a Union general's uniform to get in. In front of them was a long wide, ascending stairway. They went up the stairs, all the time looking around at the magnificence of the building. Lawrence leaned hard on his cane as he went up the plush-carpeted ornamental stairs.

Lawrence could see that Abigail was impressed with the magnitude of the building, staring at the tall ceilings above her head as she tripped on the stairs. There were three large ornate glass chandeliers hanging down, and they reflected prisms of colored lights onto the intricately woven rugs. The windows were covered in plush red velvet curtains and tied off with tasseled golden ropes. "It's so grand, Lawrence. I've never seen anything like this before," she said.

She held tight to his hand as they went up to each exhibit. Every new showcase was a wonder and a new experience for the couple. One display had the skins of a tiger and another skins of a lion.

She pulled on Lawrence's arm. "Lawrence, do you think those big cats are cold? They stripped off their coats," she said.

Lawrence laughed at her. "Abby, they don't have to worry about their skins anymore. They're dead."

"Oh. I feel sorry for them," she said. "I would have liked to have seen them alive."

Lawrence bent down and kissed her on the forehead. Her forehead felt soft against his lips. "You're sweet, honey," he said. "You're so vulnerable. I have to protect you."

White ivory tusks of a large elephant were in the hallway. And as they walked by, to their left, they saw the heads and skeletons of many large African animals; there was a gray rhinoceros skin opened up to reveal the bones inside of its body; an elephant skeleton with its massive legs, short tail, and long ivory tusks; a hippo skeleton with squat bones and a wide mouth; a giraffe with its long neck and tiny tail.

Then they went to the live exhibits. Alexander Montarg was a living skeleton. His wrists were an inch in diameter, no bigger than Lawrence's thumb. He sat on a bench and was playing the violin. While Lawrence listened, many different feelings welled up in his chest; a sense of sadness when the violin was played in a demure fashion, a shyness when it was played cautiously, and a lifting of the spirits when it was played confidently. "He plays that violin pretty good," Lawrence said. "But his chest isn't as wide as a haversack. He reminds me of the Johnny Rebs that I saw during the war, all skin and bones and starving."

After that, Abigail pushed her way through the crowd, going to the front to where Ann E. Leak was playing a grand piano. She was a Southern belle that joined *P.T. Barnum's Show* because the war had destroyed her plantation in Georgia. Lawrence inched his way through the throng and ended up standing in back of Abigail. "Look at that, Lawrence, she's got no arms," Abigail said. "She's playing the piano with her toes and turning the sheet music too."

"She's got more courage than some of the men I saw in the army," he said. "I knew a guy that was a dog robber that lost one of his arms, and he continued to still cook. But it wasn't anything that could compare to this."

Suddenly, the crowd started to melt away from the piano player. Up the stairs came Barnum's most famous person. It was General Tom Thumb. He was dressed in a black sack coat, black pants, and a beaver fur top hat. Everybody surrounded him as he walked up the hallway.

20

Abigail Meets Tom Thumb

Abigail looked in her program. And the next thing Lawrence knew, she was running toward Tom Thumb.

He walked with an air of authority, popping his little cane in front of him as he saunter toward the back of the building. Before he could get to the door that went outside, Abigail stopped him. "Mr. Thumb, would you sign my program?" she asked.

"Charles Stratton," he said.

"What?"

"My name is Charles Sherwood Stratton."

"Then would you please sign my program, Mr. Stratton?" The excitement made her hands shake.

"Sure." He signed her program with his real name first and then General Tom Thumb right under it. "You're a lovely lady." He looked up at her and smiled, and she blushed.

"Thank You."

Meanwhile, Lawrence was still standing in front of the last exhibit where Ann E. Leak was playing the piano. "Abigail, come back here for a minute, would you?" He shouted.

Abigail ran back to where Lawrence was standing. "What is it, Lawrence?" she asked.

"The lady at the piano looks so sad. Why don't you ask her for an autograph too?"

"But she has no hands," she said. Abigail felt silly having to ask the lady with no hands to give her an autograph.

"Don't worry about it, just ask her."

"Okay, if you say so." Abigail went back up to the lady and asked her for her signature. "I would be honored if you gave me your autograph, Ann." Abigail didn't know how to approach her. She hesitated and then tossed the program on the keyboard of the piano. On the big black piano were crochets of Masonic symbols; an emblem of the Knights Templar, which was a crown with a cross inside of it and a compass and a square.

"I'll write you something that you can remember and use all your life, my dear," she said.

"Can I help you, mam?" Abigail asked. She attempted to grab the pencil but was too slow. The lady had already picked it up and was writing a note.

"What's the matter, missy? Don't you think I know how to write my own name?"

"No, I just thought…" Abigail felt her embarrassment as her neck and then her face got hot.

"I know, honey," Ann said. Then she picked up the pencil with her toes as dexterously as a person that had hands would do, and wrote, "So you perceive it's really true, when hands are lacking, toes will do."

"Thank you," Abigail said. She looked at what Ann had written and then cradled the program against her chest. "I'll treasure this forever."

"You're welcome, my honey," she said. "I hope God smiles on your new marriage."

"How did you know that I was just married?" she asked.

"Your ring is new, and you carry it like it's going to break any minute. Besides, I look at people's hands a lot, not having any of my own. They tell a great deal about who the person is."

Abigail ran back to Lawrence and hugged him. "Thank you, Lawrence, for telling me to go back and see the lady. I think it made her very happy."

"I know it did," he said. "Come on, Abigail, let's go outside," Lawrence said.

"No…I want to see some more things," Abigail shouted. She started to cry like a little girl. "Can't we just stay a little bit longer?"

"Don't be so sad, honey. You're a big girl. Don't cry. We're going to the next building, five thirty-seven," Lawrence said.

"Oh, okay," Abigail said. "First, let's go see that little town over there. It says it's the city of fleas." She pulled Lawrence along until they finally stood in front of the town.

"Do you see fleas, Abigail?" Lawrence asked. He put his face close to the revolving wheels and the little red seesaws that were going up and down.

"Yeah, I do see them," she shouted. "How could all those things move without there being fleas?" She pointed at all the moving machines, convincing herself that nothing could move without something moving it.

Lawrence pulled her to the next exhibit. It was a man or possibly a machine. It was an automaton. He had a painted white face and wore white gloves and had on a derby hat. He moved with starts and stops just like a machine.

"Do you think he's a machine, Abby?" Lawrence asked.

"He sure moves like a machine." Abigail put her face close to the automaton. Then she smelled him and put her finger in his eye.

His eye began to water. "Hey, lady, don't touch the merchandise," the mechanical man said. Abigail was so startled that he spoke to her that she ran back toward Lawrence, laughing all the way.

"Well, I guess we know now he's not a machine, Abby," Lawrence said.

Next, they went by an albino boy. He had long white scraggly hair, white eyelashes, and his eyes were a deep pink. Next to him was the twenty-year-old five-hundred-pound fat lady, Hannah Perkins.

On a roundtable next to the exhibit was a crystal vase filled with red roses. Lawrence picked one up and handed it to Hannah. "Here you go, miss. A beautiful rose for a beautiful lady." She blushed, smelled the rose, and then winked at Lawrence.

"What about me?" Abigail asked. "I thought I was your only girlfriend." She walked away in a snit.

Lawrence at once, picked two roses out of the vase and handed them to her. "You're two things to me, Abigail. You're my wife, and you're my girlfriend so you get two roses."

"So you do care," Abigail asked.

"Of course, I do." She held the roses tight in her hand, and Lawrence came over, put her face in his hands, and kissed her forehead. "You feel better now?"

"Yes." She smelled the roses and chuckled. Then she looked at the gypsy fortune-teller in the corner of the room. It was a little booth and on top of it were cutouts of purple, red, and gold stars, and over them was a transparent purple curtain that went down to the floor. The door to the fortune-teller's grotto had beads strung from the top to the floor. A strange reddish glow filled the inside of the room. "Let's go there," Abigail said, pointing to the fortune-teller sitting in a chair in front of her booth.

"Do you want your fortune told?" Lawrence asked.

"No, I want her to tell your fortune."

As soon as they got close to the gypsy, she got up and asked them if they wanted their fortune told. Lawrence hesitated but was pushed from behind by Abigail toward the fortune-teller.

"Okay, okay, I'm going. Don't push me," Lawrence pleaded.

"Oh, go ahead. It'll be like she's the oracle at Delphi. She could tell us what's going to happen in the future. Wouldn't you like that?"

From the perky expression in Lawrence's eyes showing the acceptance of what she said, Abigail knew that Lawrence felt comfortable with seeing the gypsy. *He's been living in the past so much I think that this experience will be good for him*, she thought.

The next thing they knew, they were inside, sitting at a round table with a crystal ball in the middle of it. The inside of the gypsy's booth was bathed in a red sensuous light. There were golden sheer curtains hanging from the ceiling and skulls on shelves surrounding the little circular table. Lawrence put a dime in the gypsy's hand, followed by her depositing it in a secret place between her bosoms. On the table was a glass goblet filled with red wine. She took a long gulp and then smiled to herself.

Her dress hung down loose around her body, and it was multicolored with vibrant reds, blues, and greens. A babushka covered her head and was tied off by the side of her right ear. Jingling gold coins hung on a gold chain across her forehead.

"Whose fortune am I going to tell?" she asked.

"His," Abigail said as she pointed to Lawrence and laughed.

Abigail could see that Lawrence was a little bit embarrassed, and she chuckled inside to see him squirm.

Lawrence wiggled his rear end into the chair, and then he leaned on the table with his elbows and looked straight at the fortune-teller. "Well, what I want to really know is, will our young marriage last?" It was important to note that after he asked her the question, he sat back, folded his arms, and waited for the answer.

The woman rested her hands around the crystal ball while staring into it. She moaned, looked up to the ceiling, and after that, dropped her head with a thump on the table. She picked up her head and on purpose looked directly at the young couple. "Are you sure you want to hear the answer? Because what I have seen comes from the gods. I'm just a vessel that they use so that we can see future events."

"Yes, we want to know," Abigail said. "You have to tell us." She leaned forward, expecting the greatest news in her life. Lawrence reached over and squeezed her arm and smiled. Abigail wasn't sure if she believed everything that the fortune-teller told them. But it was different and exciting so she was willing to listen.

All of a sudden, the woman got up, went over to get some incense sticks and then lit them. The smell of sandalwood filled the cubicle. Inch by inch, she turned toward the couple. Abigail could see the explanation of her vision forming in her eyes.

"I saw a buck, a large deer with a set of impressive antlers, standing in a field with his harem of does. One of the deer was pregnant, and she tried to keep up with the buck but fell behind. He ran so fast through the fields that eventually he started to fly. He flew so fast and so far that he left his harem behind, including the doe that was pregnant."

Abigail became furious and stood up. "All we wanted to know was whether our marriage would last," she said.

The woman stood in the middle of the cloud of blue smoke. "It's unlikely, but it is in your power to make it happen," the woman said.

Lawrence got up all at once and turned to Abigail. "Come on, Abby, let's get out of here," he said.

"No, Lawrence, I want to hear more. I want to know what's going to happen."

"Can't you see, she's a fake?" Lawrence looked directly at the gypsy when he said that.

"Please, Lawrence, let's stay. I want to ask her more questions," she said as she cuddled up to Lawrence.

"Okay, if it will make you happy."

By this time, the gypsy had come back and was sitting at the table.

"Can I ask you more questions?" Abigail asked. Lawrence and Abigail both sat down at the same time.

"Yes, you may ask," the gypsy said, staring into the crystal ball for a vision.

"If I ask you a question and you see an image, will you tell me what the image means?" Abigail pleaded.

"I'll do my best," she said.

"It's a simple question. Does Lawrence love me?"

"Abby, you know, I love you," Lawrence interrupted.

"I know you do. I just want to hear what the gods have to say," she said.

Some time went by while the fortune-teller stared into the crystal ball. The silence was deafening and the anticipation of getting an answer from the gods was overwhelming. The woman stared blankly at the crystal ball, and then all of a sudden, she blinked her eyes, which seemed to bring her back to the living. "I have an image that was given to me. Do you want to know what it was?"

"Yes," the young couple said at the same time.

"I saw two men in Greek armor with swords and shields fighting one another. A woman standing at a distance away was crying and telling them to stop, but they wouldn't. Finally, one of the men killed the other. He went over to the woman and told her to lie down in his shield. She did. He tied ropes to his shield and pulled her back to his camp."

"But that still doesn't tell me if Lawrence loves me," Abigail shouted.

"What the vision tells me is that he doesn't love you immediately, but much more likely will with time." Whether it was a coincidence or the gypsy saw something in the young girl that made her talk about the Greek soldiers, Abigail would never know. Although, as ridiculous as it might seem, she accepted what the fortune-teller told her as true messages from the gods.

"This is ridiculous, Abby. Now for the second time let's get out of here!" Lawrence shouted.

Abigail could see that Lawrence was becoming impatient and that he wanted to leave, but she had a question that just had to be answered.

"Just one more question and then we'll go," Abigail said. "Will they find Burton?"

"Abigail, that's enough," Lawrence whispered.

With that, the fortune-teller draped a purple silk handkerchief over the crystal ball. Then she lifted up one side of the hanky and stared at the clear solid globe of glass inside. While Abigail stared at the lady, she could have swore that her eyes turned a bright blue.

A minute later, she whipped the handkerchief off the crystal ball and stuffed it up for sleeve.

"Well, what did you see?" Abigail asked.

"You understand now that these images may not make sense to you, but it is what I've seen. I'll try to interpret what I have seen, but as I've said before, it is what I think it means."

"Yes…yes…I understand what you're saying. Now what did you see?" Abigail asked. She leaned forward so that she could hear everything.

"I saw a man in gold armor with a sword in his hand facing an enemy. The enemies were women and looked Oriental or Persian, I'm not sure. All of a sudden, the women grew in stature until they looked like giants. But the man in the gold armor was not afraid. He just hollered up at the giants, daring them to fight. But the giants were afraid and backed away from the fight. The man began to laugh, and suddenly, a spear went through his back, and he collapsed on the ground. The next image was of a burning pyre with his body on top of it, being consumed by the flames. Then a ghostly image floated from his body and quickly dissolved into the ground. That's all I saw."

"And just what does that mean," Abigail asked as she leaned forward.

The gypsy took another large swig of the wine. "I'm not sure. You'll have to make your own interpretation," the fortune-teller said. "There are some visions better left alone. Our session is over."

Lawrence got up first and went back out the door. Abigail followed close behind. They met up next to the entrance of the booth.

"What do you think?" Abigail asked. She moved close to Lawrence for comfort.

"I think it's a lot of hooey," Lawrence said. "Nobody can see into the future, least of all, that woman. She's a con artist. Let's skedaddle out of here, Abby."

"Okay. You looked so mad when you got up and left that I thought we were going to leave forever," she said.

"No. I just want to get away from this fortune-telling booth," he said as he walked towards the stairs.

As they got to the top of the landing, a giant of a woman was walking up the stairs. It was Anna Swan, and she was over seven feet eleven inches tall. Abigail stopped in her tracks with her mouth open and looked up at the gigantic lady. "Am I dreaming, Lawrence? Pinch me, will ya."

"No, I see the same thing you do. She's real."

"Do you think that's the kind of giant that the gypsy saw in her vision?" Abigail asked.

"I don't think so, Abby. She's just a freak of nature," he said as he looked up at the woman.

As Anna walked by, she looked down at them, smiled and nodded her head. "Hello," she said. "Welcome to the American Museum." Then it seemed that she took only a few huge steps to reach a hallway that was on the other side of the building and she was gone.

After Anna passed by the couple, they went back down the stairs and out the door toward the building that was attached to the museum. It was building 537 and on top of it, etched into the stone of the building in big letters was Van Amburg's menagerie. In the front of the building was a large plate glass window that allowed people to look in from the street upon the wild animals. Abigail had the lead and ended up looking through the window first.

What she saw made her doubt her sanity. She thought she was in a dream, but even more than that were the words that came to mind from the little red book that she had just read. The strange children's book called *Alice's Adventures in Wonderland* was filled with outlandish characters and talking animals, a white rabbit, a dormouse, a caterpillar, and the strangest of all, was a Cheshire cat. She wondered if the uncertain feeling that she had about what was real and what wasn't was the way things appeared to Lawrence when he had his attacks.

The book brought to mind what Alice had said:

> "But I don't want to go among mad people," Alice remarked.
>
> "Oh, you can't help that," said the cat. "We're all mad here. I'm mad. You're mad."
>
> "How do you know I'm mad?" asked Alice.
>
> "You must be," said the cat, "or you wouldn't have come here."

Abigail pressed her nose against the plate-glass window. Inside were a white-and-black striped zebra; camels leaning up against the cage, scratching their humps; llamas, their distant cousins, constantly chewing their cuds; kangaroos with their joeys poking their heads out of their pouches; hyenas jerking in their bellies every time they laughed; and white plodding polar bears being thrown fish and stepping on them with their front paws as they pulled off the skin. Of course, she had seen these animals before but only in her mind's eye. She had read about them in books. But now they were real, chomping on oats, fish, or red pieces of meat.

"Come on, Abigail, we better get in there, or we'll miss the show," Lawrence said. "You'll see better things inside during the performance." He put his arm through the crook of her arm, and they walked to their seats. Abigail sat directly in front of Lawrence.

The lights dimmed in the auditorium and then a round beam of light penetrated the cage that was set up in the distance. Suddenly, a man appeared dressed in a gladiatorial Roman toga. He carried a whip with him and snapped it into the air above his head. Abigail quickly looked into her program. "He's known as the Lion King," she said. "Is that Van Amburg?" Abigail asked as she leaned forward to get a better look.

"Yep, I think that's him," Lawrence said.

Suddenly, three male lions trotted into the cage and then proceeded to sit on the individual platforms. They all had large, thick furry manes. They roared, tipped their heads, and showed their white fangs. The lion tamer twirled the whip above his head which seemed to be a signal for the cats to sit on their hind legs and then to reach up and paw the sky.

Everyone clapped. Then the lion tamer bowed to the crowd. He walked over to each lion and touched each one on the nose. They sat still, not moving a muscle. After that, he went to the middle of the cage and called them. They immediately came to him and lay down in front of him. All this time, he did not have to crack the whip. They followed his instructions as if they were docile kittens.

"Simba," he said, commanding the largest of the lions to sit by his side. He reached in with both hands and opened up the lion's mouth, followed by him putting his arm into the lion's open jaws. The audience gasped and some of the women fainted.

"Are you okay, Abigail," Lawrence asked as he put his hand on her shoulder.

"Oh, I'm all right." She responded to Lawrence without even turning around. Her eyes were glued to the spectacle in front of her. How can he do that? She thought. He must be mean to them. That's why they do what he tells them. They do it out of fear, not respect. If he's not careful, they'll forget their fear and eat him.

Then he followed that with an even more dangerous feat. He put his head into the mouth of the big cat. Again, many of the women shrieked and hid their faces in their hankies, but secretly, with bated breath, they were enraptured by the demonstration.

Abigail had her hands in front of her face, but she looked through the openings in her fingers. When that demonstration was over, he opened the door of the cage that allowed the lions, except for one lonely lion, to leave into another cage. They seemed happy to get away. Abigail could swear that she saw an expression of relief on their faces as they left the arena. She imagined them looking at each other and saying, "I'm glad that's over. I don't have to be humiliated anymore." *After all, they were the king of beasts*, she thought.

Then the next thing that the lion tamer did surprised Abigail beyond anything she could imagine. A small cage door opened at the other end of the arena and a small white lamb trotted out. Van Amburg, the bravest lion tamer she had ever seen, picked up the innocent little animal and walked over to the snarling lion. Abigail feared that he was going to feed the little lamb to the reclining lion. Low and behold, that was what he was about to do.

The women around her shrieked, and some of them hollered out loud, "Nooooo." Abigail got up from her seat to get a better look. Even though she was afraid to look at what she thought was going to happen, she couldn't help herself. She reached back and grabbed Lawrence's arm for support, all the while still looking at the cage. There was silence in the arena, not as much as a cough or clearing of the throat could be heard. The air was filled with thick electricity, a frightening vibration.

Van Amburg, with the lamb in his arms, walked over to the lion. He immediately put the lamb in between the lion's paws. Then he walked away. The lion sniffed at the lamb and then opened its jaws. Everyone in the arena gasped. Everyone's eyes were wide and mouths open. Screams were heard, and the shuffling commotion of people beside themselves, stamping their feet, banging their canes on the floor, and exploding into a rowdy mob.

All at once the lion licked the lamb affectionately. This was so much different than what the multitude expected that there was a long silence. And then the crowd broke out in cheers, and whistles, and the stamping of their feet on the bleachers. After that shock, a collective sigh went through the crowd.

As soon as the lion had gone, Van Amburg had picked up the lamb, and put it back in its protective little cage. Not a second later, ten-striped tigers—all brown and black striped—were introduced into the enclosure. They lay down in a row; the lion tamer whirled his whip into the air and grunted. They all turned over in unison.

"Well, you got your wish, Abigail," Lawrence said.

"What do you mean?"

"You wanted to see them alive, didn't you?" Lawrence put his hands on her shoulders. She touched his hand to reassure him and to thank him.

"You can say that again," she said. "They sure are alive."

Next, the lion tamer set two steal hoops on fire. The tigers clawed at the air and growled in his face because it seemed they were more afraid of the fire than they were of him. He snapped the whip and drove the tigers through the large rings. When they got through the hoops and onto the platforms on the other side, they continued growling and pawing at the flames.

He whirled his whip over his head; it made a whooshing sound through the air. The Tigers jumped down off their platforms and sat. He kept whirling his whip through the air which made the tigers hop the length of the cage on their hind legs. Then the show was over. People filed out of the building onto the street. It was ten or eleven o'clock by now, but Abigail did not want to go home, or to go back to the hotel.

21

FOOD FIT FOR A KING OR QUEEN

"WELL, MRS. ELLSWORTH, where do you want to go now?" Lawrence asked.

"I'm so hungry I could eat a horse," Abigail said, looking around for some place to eat.

"How about this place, Abby?" he asked, pointing to a restaurant right next door to the museum.

"I don't care, just as long as they have food," she said.

"How about if we eat in a place I heard of called Delmonico's?" Lawrence asked. He swore that he heard Abigail's stomach growl. "Did I hear your stomach growl?"

"You sure did," she said. "Okay, okay, let's go to that Delmonico's place just as long as they serve food."

"Driver, driver," Lawrence shouted into the street in the direction of an omnibus. The driver was racing down Broadway in a fury, directing the horses away from any pedestrians in the road or carriages that might stop his progress. The bus driver seemed as if he was possessed by a ferocious spirit. He suddenly skidded to a halt in front of Abigail and Lawrence. Lawrence was afraid for Abigail so he pulled her closer to his side.

"Whoa!" he shouted. "Well, Billy Yank, where are you goin?" he asked. He had a thick Irish Brogue. He wore a loose-fitting, boxy coat with loose pants and a waistcoat. The waistcoat was flowered brocade and matching. His thick black curly hair popped out from under his bowler hat.

"We're going to Delmonico's," Lawrence said.

"There's good eats dere," he said. "You'd be an arse not to love their food."

"That's what I hear," Lawrence said as he and Abigail walked up the stairs and sat in their seats. "It's between Beaver and William Street, isn't it?"

"Yep," the driver said. Then he snapped the whip over the horses. "Getty up," he shouted. The bus lurched forward and picked up speed. The street opened up into a wide boulevard and people were moving in every direction, but most of all, they were heading toward Broadway. Many of the four-story buildings had awnings hanging over the cobblestone sidewalks. There were butcher stores, art stores, furniture stores, and stores that dealt in anything one could think of. Their lights streamed through their windows, illuminating a path through the darkness of the night.

Lawrence could see that Abigail took in the sights of this new world like a sponge, and occasionally, she would reach up and feel for the necklace and earrings to see if they were still there.

There are so many people, so many things, so much to see, so much she could learn, he thought. The people rush down the sidewalks possibly in search of something new, something not purchased, something that would give their lives some color and excitement. Even through the darkness, Lawrence could see the happy faces and hear the laughter of the people; a woman was towing her children behind her, three sailors with bottles of beer in their hands were clapping each other on the back, and a rich woman in a luxurious carriage was fanning herself. The clatter of the omnibus and the clip clop of the horses made Lawrence whisper close to Abigail's ear.

"Boy, we're going fast, aren't we, Abigail?" he asked her while she held tight to his waist. At that moment, the omnibus stopped clattering over cobblestones because it was running through a marsh and up a hill, which made it slow to a crawl. The wheels made a squishy sucking sound as they sank deep into the mud and muck. "Ah…that's better. At least now, we can see what were driving past."

"You're right, Lawrence."

The omnibus again went back onto a paved cobblestone road which brought it back into the heart of the city onto a street that ran between three- and four-story buildings. And for some unexplained reason, the driver slowed up through the most impoverished section of the city.

The smell of rotting garbage and the site of the wagon wheels running through the refuse thrown on the streets made Lawrence sick to his stomach, making it roll like a rowboat on high seas. Filth of every kind was thrown into the streets—dead dogs, cats, and rats littered the side of the road. Manure from the horses settled in steaming piles and vegetable refuse rotted. And it seemed that the garbage boxes were rarely emptied.

In between some of the apartment buildings, in spaces no wider than forty inches, people had made the openings their homes. They had put wood over the gaps to form a roof to cover them from the rain; children wrapped in filth and barely clothed lay on the streets, in doorways, and in front of their makeshift dwellings. These sad dwellings were called rear houses, where only the poorest families lived.

"How can people live like that, Lawrence?" Abigail asked.

"Most of these people are immigrants. I don't think many of them can even speak English," Lawrence said. They passed by tenement buildings with women outside hanging their white linens stretched across the sides of the buildings; their children hanging on to their skirts and babies being carried, crying into their ears. Black soot billowed out of the chimneys and covered the buildings with a brown skin.

"Aren't you glad we don't live here?" she asked Lawrence.

"Nice place to visit, but I wouldn't want to make my home here," Lawrence said. "There's as many freaks out here on the streets as there were in Barnum's Museum." In his heart, he couldn't understand why he was so insensitive to these people's situation. *After all*, he thought, *these are people too*. But then he realized why, and it was because they seemed like invaders to him—these immigrants from another land; these people who didn't even speak English. At least the rebs were from this country.

"Yes," she whispered to Lawrence.

Then the omnibus went down the hill through a marshland with the horses splashing through the water and into an overgrown meadow, followed by it going down a dusty road to only wind up again on a cobblestone street. They eventually ended up in a part of the city that was more businesslike with well-kept streets and modern four-story buildings on each side of the boulevard.

"Here we is folks," the driver shouted as he pulled up in front of Delmonico's restaurant. "Don't fart around. There's a line formin' already," he said.

Over the front door in bold letters chiseled into the marble was the word Delmonico's. It had beautiful iron balconies, and in the marble entrance portico, there were four columns from Pompeii. The building was known as the Citadel because of the unique rounded corner. Lounging around its entrance was a cross section of the natives of New York City and other people as far as one could tell from somewhere else—merchants, Southerners smoking Havana's, tall Western cowboys with their ten-gallon hats, and exotic-looking women with their well-dressed gentleman escorts.

Lawrence and Abigail got out of the omnibus as quickly as they could and then stood in line waiting to get in. Lawrence leaned heavily on his cane.

"Lawrence, I'm starving," Abigail said as she rubbed her belly. "How long do you think we'll have to stand in line before we can get something to eat?"

"I don't know," Lawrence said. "Let's just wait a little longer and see if the line gets a little shorter."

Just as Lawrence was saying that, Abigail leaned out into the road and looked down the length of the line to see how long it was. Suddenly, a circular front coupe carriage came barreling around the corner and struck Abigail, throwing her to the curb.

"Abby...Abby, are you all right?" Lawrence asked as he picked her up under her arms.

"I'm okay," she said. He could see that she was more surprised than hurt.

The driver of the carriage jumped down off the carriage and quickly ran over to Abigail and Lawrence. "I'm sorry, miss. I didn't see you. Are you all right?" He attempted to help Lawrence pick Abigail up and in the process lost his top hat.

"It's okay. I've got her," Lawrence said as he picked her up. It was then that he realized how petite and light she was.

The door of the carriage opened up and a small built man with a suit on, a little black tie, a black top hat, and an ornate gold top cane stepped out of the carriage. An air of authority surrounded him as he approached Lawrence and Abigail.

"I'ma sorry, madam. Mi-a driver went da to fast. Pa-pa-please accept my apology," he said.

Even though he talked in broken English, the couple could see that he was truly sorry from the way he took his hat off and stared up at the couple. The top of his head was bald, and he had lamb chop sideburns. His blue eyes were kind.

"Mi namea is Lorenzo. Ma, mi relative and me own disa restaurant," he said. "I'd be honorda if you would be mi guest free of charge forta dinner."

"Why yes. Thank you," Abigail said. "I've got to get something to eat or I'm going to die."

"Splendid a," Lorenzo said. "Follow may." He led the couple to the side of the structure and through the kitchen. Abigail slid as she went into the bowls of the building because there was grease on the floor. She caught herself by grabbing hold of a stainless steel table. There were men dressed in white aprons—some sitting, some running around—but all with food either being prepared by them or being transported into the dining room.

Lawrence knew the smell of garlic, oregano, onion, and steak being seared, wine being added to the food, and the odor of pungent spices hanging in the atmosphere would drive Abigail crazy. In his imagination, he saw himself cutting a slice out of the air and devouring it. Even the steam from the large pots smelled strangely like olives.

Before Lorenzo brought the couple to the dining room, he stopped off at the cashier sitting at the entrance to the building. He kissed her and then said something in what seemed to be Italian.

"Lawrence, why did he kiss that cashier?" Abigail asked. "Does he kiss all the help?"

Lawrence laughed. "I think that's his wife."

"I've never heard of women having such power," she said.

He returned, and the couple followed him past a large dining room with parquet floors that was filled with women sitting around individual tables. It was the meeting of a local group of book lovers that had gathered to discuss their latest reading. Before Delmonico's started the tradition of women entering such a place unescorted, it was taboo for women to be alone.

"Here we go," Lorenzo said as he pointed to a table against the wall.

"Can we have a table far away from the door but facing it and with our back against the wall?" Lawrence asked.

"Surely," Lorenzo said.

"Why do you want the table over there?" Abigail asked. "Sometimes I don't understand you." She had a frown on her face as she walked next to Lawrence.

"It's to keep us safe so nobody can sneak up behind us, and so I can see whoever is coming into the restaurant," Lawrence said, looking at the door while passing by it.

The dining room radiated magnificence. They were led into a room that had deep-pile carpets and damask draperies framing the windows. The glass light in the chandeliers were softly shaded, so as Abigail looked up at them, she crashed into one of the red-cushioned chairs.

The round table had immaculate snow-white tablecloths draped over it. The couple sat down at their own private table, and Lawrence reached out and rubbed the palms of his hands over the smooth surface. The plates were edged in dark red with a white center and the letter D etched in the middle, with a fork to the left and a knife to the right. A large white napkin sat on a small white dish to the side of the main plate. A large glass goblet with a smaller one next to it dominated the middle of the table. A small white oil lamp with a white shade beamed a soft glow to the surface. In the very center of the table was a crystal vase with red roses in it.

Lawrence picked up the large red menu which had no less than three hundred and fifty items in it. As he turned the pages, the steaks and all that went with them caught his eye.

"How about steak and potatoes, Abby?" he asked.

"That's fine."

The waiters seemed that they read Abigail's mind since they put a basket of Italian bread on the table in front of her with little pats of butter in a dish next to it. She ravenously tore off a piece of bread and then buttered it. She tore into it with a smile. Her eyes shined as she chewed with delight. "Oh, that's so good," she spoke softly to Lawrence. "It's warm too." She broke off a little piece of bread, no larger than a communion wafer, and slathered a pat of butter on it and leaned over to Lawrence. "Open up," she demanded. Then she slipped it onto his tongue.

"It's good, Abby," he said. It was chewy with a hint of garlic infused in the crust of the bread.

The couple was besieged with waiters coming and going. It seemed to Lawrence that anything they wanted, they could have just for the asking. He talked to one of the waiters as he rushed by, "Hey, who's that Lorenzo?"

The waiter stopped in his tracks and turned to face Lawrence. "Why, he's the man that started this whole restaurant," he said. "Is there anything else I can help you with, sir?"

Lawrence's mouth watered even as he was ordering the meal. "We'll have the Delmonico steaks and the special potatoes. And for dessert, we want the baked Alaska."

"I want my dessert now, Lawrence," Abigail said.

"Well, you heard the lady. I'll have my dessert now too."

The waiter leaned forward over the table as if he was bowing to his customers. "Will that be all?" he asked.

"No, no!" Abigail shouted. "We want your best champagne. Please bring it with the dessert."

"As you wish," the attendant said and then he was off in a flash.

Not five minutes later, three waiters paraded out of the kitchen. One of the servers had a large bucket filled with ice with the champagne bottle sitting in the middle of it. The other two waiters carried their desserts.

The wine waiter wrapped the white napkin around the bottle and popped the cork. The sound of the cork was so much like the shot of muskets that it made Lawrence jump. He quickly held himself together so as not to show his fear. A small amount of champagne was poured into Lawrence's goblet. "Is that to your liking, sir?"

"Don't I get any more than that?" Lawrence asked with a frown on his face.

"I was just wondering if you like the bouquet and the taste of the champagne. That's why I poured just a little in the glass."

"Oh, I see what you're saying," Lawrence said as he felt his neck and face get hot from his embarrassment. He put the goblet to his nose and then sipped a little bit of the bubbly liquid. He waved the goblet in front of the waiter and said, "Fill 'er up, good man." Then he smiled a big smile at Abigail.

"Me too," Abigail demanded as she waved her goblet in front of the waiter. The attendant poured the champagne in her glass with a little twist at the end so that it wouldn't drip.

After that, the other two servers put the desserts in front of Abigail and Lawrence.

"What's this?" Lawrence asked. In front of him sat a round and pointed golden-brown meringue. "This looks like a sea urchin."

"That's your baked Alaska, sir," the attendant said.

Lawrence looked at the dessert from every angle. He even got up out of his chair and looked at the top of it. "Okay. Let's give it a try," he said as he cut off a piece with the edge of his fork. The slice consisted of meringue, Devil's food cake, and ice cream. Then he lifted his fork up and looked at it from underneath. Finally, he put it in his mouth and savored it. "Oh my god. I never tasted anything like this in my life." It tasted creamy and like bananas and like vanilla meringue with a touch of rum. All the flavors blended together in the ice cream and cake. "Try it, Abby."

Abigail cut off a large piece with her fork and held onto it with her fingers so it wouldn't drop off. Then she stuffed it into her mouth. "I think I died and went to heaven," she said. "That's so good." She leaned back in her chair and looked up at the ceiling.

The couple delighted in their dessert, and every time they toasted each other, they gulped down a large mouthful of champagne. Lawrence was getting drunk and could hardly sit up straight in his chair. Without Lawrence recognizing it, the maître d' leaned over his left shoulder and put the stake in front of him. "Can I get you anything else, sir?" he asked.

"No, I don't think so. Does Abigail have her steak?" he asked.

"Oh yes, she does."

Lawrence dipped a large soup spoon into the potato casserole that was in the middle of the table and then put some on Abigail's plate. And in turn, put some on his own dish. He sampled the potatoes; there was the taste of cheese, half and half and butter. And on top it was covered in breadcrumbs. It was creamy and smooth, and the potatoes were cooked to perfection.

He looked over at Abigail, and all she could do because she was so overwhelmed by the tastes and smells of the food was to keep eating and shaking her head back and forth saying, "I can't believe how good this is."

The smell of the steak wafted up into Lawrence's nose. It smelled slightly sweet, buttery, and smoky all at the same time. There were red blood juices oozing out of the bottom of the steak, making a bloody soup surrounding the dark charcoal meat. He cut a piece about the size of a large crouton and then popped it into his mouth. It had a beefy smoked crispy flavor and was moist and juicy. It was the best meat he had ever tasted.

The only thing that could have enhanced his enjoyment of eating this chunk of meat was for him to imagine that he was the hunter who brought back this food for his family. While he chewed, that is exactly what he thought and it made it taste even better.

But all of a sudden, Lawrence's stomach turned over. The smell of the meat that was so mouthwatering once now triggered a buried memory of the smell of burning flesh.

He fought against the smell by putting his nose in the large goblet filled with champagne. As he breathed the smell of alcohol into his lungs, the burning-flesh odor in his mind faded away. He felt proud of himself because he had defeated one of the demons that he had brought back from the war.

In contrast to this luxurious meal, he remembered the large quantities of stale beef or salt horse as they called it served out and also rusty unwholesome pork and hard tack biscuits that they had to endure in the army. There was ham, hard bread, potatoes, and the occasional onion, dried apples, dried peaches, coffee, tea, sugar, and molasses.

But he could only think of these foods as fuel for the human machine to keep it going, to keep it as alert as possible, to keep it as a killing contraption. We were like the automaton that we saw today. The way we marched in a row on the battlefield shoulder to shoulder like machines, the way we waited for the bullets to pierce our flesh, the way we did it over and over again never learning to stop the insanity. *Quite the reverse, we never learned from our mistakes, we kept marching into the horror*, he thought.

"You're kind of quiet over there, Abigail," Lawrence said as he stopped eating.

"I'm too busy stuffin' my face," Abigail said.

With both of their stakes gone from the plates, it was time, Lawrence thought, *to try something else from the menu.* "Hay, fella, come over here will ya?" Lawrence asked.

The maître d' walked over to the table and stood there with his hands clasped behind his back waiting for his orders. He reminded Lawrence of a recruit standing at attention. "Yes, sir, can I help you?"

"Let me see the menu again," Lawrence commanded. The list of food was so overwhelming that he closed his eyes and ordered whatever his finger landed on. When he opened his eyes again, he smiled because fate had ordered sweets for them. "Oh, that looks good, let's both have a piece of coconut cream pie, a piece of apple pie, and put a scoop of strawberry ice cream on the plate too."

"As you wish, sir." Then the server scooted away into the kitchen as if he was being nudged along by a devil. A minute later, he came out with the desserts. He put them in front of the couple. He bent down close to Lawrence. "Will that be all, sir?" he asked.

"Yes, this is fine."

"Oh no, Lawrence. I couldn't eat another bite," Abigail said as she looked down at the pies. Then after staring at the dessert a while, she said, "Maybe just a taste." This time, she grabbed a large spoon and scooped up a bit of each pie and a dollop of ice cream.

Lawrence laughed out loud. "Did you have enough to eat?" he asked. The smell of the cinnamon and spice in the hot apple pie drifted up into his face.

"Oh yeah."

Immediately, after that the servers poured coffee into their cups and refilled their glasses with ice water.

Lawrence slumped back in his chair and closed his eyes. Every muscle in his body relaxed, every feeling of hunger that he ever had was wiped away. Not only the hunger in his stomach, but the hunger for contentment and the absence of fear was also satiated. He hung his arms over the sides of the chair and stretched out his legs. He was beyond a doubt satisfied.

"Lawrence," Abigail said as she sipped her coffee. "I don't want you to think that I'm ungrateful about you taking me to New York and showing me that there's a big wonderful world beyond the farm. But I want to go home now. I want to see my Pa and smell the new earth after Noah plows the fields with Rebel. And taste our simple food again."

"You aren't happy we came here to this big city and to the Barnum Museum?"

"Oh no. Don't misunderstand me, my darling," she said. "I'll remember this trip for the rest of my life. I had no idea that such strange people and such exotic animals existed. When I look back at this complicated city of tall buildings and its thousands of people, I appreciate our little farm. They all seem like they're fighting against each other just to survive." She poured a little cream into her coffee, took another sip, put her cup down in the saucer, and rested her elbows on the table.

"Okay. I understand," he said. But the truth of the matter was that Lawrence didn't understand. His feelings were hurt as he listened to Abigail. *How could she say that after all the things I did for her*, he thought, *but even more than that he envied her for finding herself in the midst of all the excitement of the last two days.*

"I'm not sophisticated like the women parading on the streets with their big fancy hats and flowing dresses. I'm just a simple farm girl that's become hypnotized by the glitter."

"I'll send Daniel a telegram as soon as we get back to Connecticut so he can meet us at the dock tomorrow," Lawrence said, pushing out his seat and throwing his napkin on the table.

"What's wrong, Lawrence, you seem upset?" Abigail motioned to the waiters to take all the dirty dishes off the table.

"I'm your husband, I should be making a decision whether to go or not," he said. "Is this how the rest of the marriage is going to be? You'll be the boss, and I'll be the slave?" A seething hatred for her exploded in his belly. He suddenly got up so quickly that he rattled the dishes on the table. He grabbed a knife next to his plate and walked over to Abigail and pointed it at her throat.

"Lawrence...Lawrence, what are you doing?" she shouted. "It's Abigail."

All of a sudden, he felt as if he were falling and waking up at the same time. He fluttered his eyes and shook his head. Then he looked at the knife in his hand. "Oh my god, what was I going to do?" He dropped the knife on the table; it clanked on the dishes.

"Are you all right, Lawrence?" Abigail asked, slumping down into the chair.

"I'm all right now." He kneeled down next to Abigail, put his head on her lap and said, "I'm sorry. I'm so sorry. I don't know what came over me, I couldn't control myself."

This incident even surprised Lawrence. One minute, he was sitting at the opposite end of the table, and the next minute, he knew he had the knife at Abigail's throat.

Abigail caressed Lawrence's hair. "It's all right. No harm done," she said.

As he lay on her lap, he could feel her trembling with fear. He wished he could take back what had just happened, but it was too late. It was as if it were somebody else, as though someone had stolen his body and his mind and was doing what they wished with it.

The maître d' walked cautiously up to the couple. "Is there anything I can do for you?" he asked.

"No," Abigail said.

"Are you done and ready to leave?" he asked.

"Yes," she said.

"Then would you be so gracious as to let us take you home?"

"You would do that for us?" By this time, Lawrence had gotten off Abigail's lap and was standing next to her chair.

"Yes, madam, Lorenzo would be honored if you let us take you home in his private carriage," he said. "This way please."

22

THE LONG RIDE HOME

THE COUPLE SLOWLY followed the maître d' to the back of the building where the carriage was waiting. The door of the carriage was opened and they stepped inside. It was lined with red plush velvet carpeting and the windows had tassels hanging down in front of them.

"Where to, sir?" the driver shouted from his seat on top of the carriage.

"To the Grand Hotel on Broadway and W. Thirty-First Street," Lawrence said. The couple was cradled in each other's arms as the carriage brought them to the hotel. It pulled up in front of the seven-story building, and they got out. It was past midnight, and they were both exhausted. But for Lawrence, the challenge of going up to the room was not over.

"I'm so tired I could sleep for a week," Abigail said. "Let's go to our room, Lawrence." Abigail ran up the stairs of the entrance to the hotel and into the lobby. Then she ran up the first flight of stairs and sat on the top landing waiting for Lawrence.

This same scene was repeated seven times. It was a Herculean feat for Lawrence to go up the stairs. He grunted and groaned, shifted his weight from side to side, and grabbed onto the railings to help himself. Finally, they reached their room. Abigail unlocked the door, and they both flopped onto the bed exhausted. "We'll meet Daniel tomorrow on the dock. He should be there," Lawrence said, talking into his pillow.

The couple slept the sleep of the dead. Their bodies were in the same position as they were when they collapsed on the bed. Lawrence was the first to wake up. He swung his legs over the side of the bed and sat up. He smacked his lips because it felt like he had a mouth full of cotton and then massaged his face. He was groggy and struggled to go over to the door of the apartment; pulling it open, he looked down the hallway. There so happened to be a bellboy in the passageway. The boy was dressed in a military-type blue uniform. "Hello, son. Would you take my luggage down stairs and put it in a carriage? We're leaving to go to the dock," Lawrence said.

"Yes, Mr. Ellsworth. I would be happy to do that for you," he said.

"How did you know my name?" Lawrence asked.

"We know all of our customers' names, sir," the boy said. The bags sat on the floor unopened. He came into the room with the little cart and piled the luggage on it.

"Wake up, Abby, it's time to go home," Lawrence said. He shook her on the shoulder. The gentleness and tolerance that he once displayed to her before and after the wedding was now a faded memory.

"Oh good," she said. "I've had enough excitement to last me a lifetime." She went over to the wash basin, poured herself some water, and washed her face. "I'm ready."

"I'll meet you downstairs, Abby. I'll be along in a minute," Lawrence said. Abigail scurried out of the room and down the stairs.

Lawrence looked out the window of the room to the street below. He had never been in a building that was seven stories high. He wondered if this was how God saw us when he looked down at the hustle and bustle of the flawed creatures that he had created. The people on the sidewalk looked like little mechanical dolls as they peddled on their bicycles, as they ran down the streets, as they scurried across the cobblestone road, and as they whipped their horses.

Lawrence found that going down the stairs was easier than going up. He grabbed hold of the rail and slid down with the help of his loose grip, opening his hand now and then when he had to negotiate the steps on the way down.

When he got to the bottom of the stairs, Abigail was already there, relaxing in a red plush high-backed chair. She was talking to the young boy that had brought down their bags, laughing and enjoying his company.

"I see you forgot about me didn't you, Abigail?" he said. "You weren't lonely, your new boyfriend with the two strong legs kept you company."

"I was just talking to him. What's wrong?" Abigail asked. "He's just a boy."

"About your age, isn't he," Lawrence said. "Maybe you'd rather be with a whole boy rather than a half man."

"I don't know what you mean," Abigail said.

No more was said about the incident on the way to the dock. They sat in the carriage getting bumped and jostled in their seats without saying a word to each other. Even after they got to their cabin and had stored their luggage under their bed, there was no communication.

Lawrence went out on deck while Abigail stayed in the cabin. He looked out at the expanse of ocean, the swelling, the chafing, the fury, and the endless disappearance over the horizon, the realization that it gave no quarter to neither man nor beast. It was without a light to guide your way, or a port to set your anchor. Even in the light of day, it was still night under the lapping waves. He thought this great expanse was like his mind struggling to understand itself. All of a sudden, he put his forehead on the railing and sobbed. He banged on his skull with his fist, wishing he could reach into his brain and pull out the malignant thing that lived there.

He turned and saw a deck chair pushed up against the ship so he flopped down on it, placed his hands on the back of his head and looked out toward the dark ocean. Then he turned on his side and watched the spray from the sea cascade over the deck. It felt good on his face and he didn't mind that it made him wet with salty water. In the distance was the low bellow of a foghorn and under him was the *thump, thump, thump* of the engines.

All at once, he felt Abigail in back of him, pressing her belly and thighs against his back. "Is that my girlfriend Lily, or my wife Abigail?" he asked. They both chuckled.

"No, it's your girlfriend Abigail," she whispered softly in his ear.

"If we keep our hope and optimism alive, we'll beat this together, Abigail." He held her hand that was around his waist and talked into the air without turning around.

She talked to the back of his head. "I was afraid. I didn't know what to say to make you feel better so I didn't say anything."

Lawrence turned back toward Abigail and placed her head on his chest. "I know how hard it is for you to see me this way, possessed by so many demons, and unable to get away from them," he said as he kissed her on the forehead. "We'll be back home in a couple hours, or at least back in Connecticut." They lay in each other's arms for the rest of the voyage.

She looked up at Lawrence. "We can't fight for love like men do," she said. "We have to be chased and wooed. I think that's how nature designed it, just like the male animals chase the females."

"I think you're right, Abby," he said. "Maybe that's why men start wars…to clear the way to chase after their women."

The pulse of the engines slowed and the ship glided into the dock in the Connecticut harbor. It was noon when they tied up to the wharf and went down the gangplank and over to the telegraph office. Just as Lawrence went to open the door, he noticed Daniel sitting next to the building.

"Daniel," Lawrence hollered. "I didn't expect to see you here. I was just going to telegraph you." He walked over to the carriage.

"Oh, Mister Lawrence, I never went back to the farm. I just stayed around here and waited for youz' to come back."

"I'm glad you did, Daniel," Lawrence said as he patted him on the back. Daniel got out of the buckboard and went over and helped Lawrence with the luggage. Then they all got in the wagon, and Lawrence slapped the reins over Rebel's flanks, and they were headed back home.

"Lawrence, can we go back home a different way?" Abigail asked at the same time as she tugged on the sleeve of his shirt.

"Sure, Abby," he said while snapping the whip over the horse to get it to trot faster. "The road is a little bit rougher, but it'll get us back home quicker."

Not a mile away from the shore, they ran into stands of red maples, aspens, white paper birch, and oak-hickory forests. Between the pine forests, there were sandy savannas with low growing shrubs. The maples were majestic against the blue sky as were the oak-chestnut forests. Even this early in September, the leaves were turning rusty brown, light yellow, and crimson.

The blue jays screamed through the oaks as they attacked the gray squirrels scampering down the trunks of the trees. All these sights and sounds were familiar to them all. Rebel trotted a little bit faster without being coaxed, knowing somehow that he was headed home. "Look at those jays going after that squirrel," Abigail said, pointing at the tree.

"Whoa, Rebel," Lawrence shouted, pulling up hard on the reins to avoid a wild turkey that ran in front of the horse. The bird let out a loud gobble at the same time that it went down a ravine and into the woods. "Home sweet home. The animals that we know so well are saying hello."

"Eyes bet you never saw any of these animals in New York," Daniel said.

"No, none of these kinds of creatures. But we did see human animals that would make you shake your head and wonder if you were dreaming." Lawrence and Abigail looked at each other and laughed.

"Getty up," Lawrence shouted while snapping the reins over the horse's rump. They were off again toward home. Although after two hours of trying to stay on the trail, the sun turned dull behind milky clouds and then became a grayish-yellow wafer. The clouds drizzled a cold rain on the three travelers. Abigail and Daniel were still asleep.

But Lawrence's body, being the perfect barometer of the weather that it was, forewarned him of the coming storm. His foot ached, and the pain traveled up his leg pricking at him, making him remember when he wanted to forget. He wondered if his pain was a gift or curse. After all, it seemed to give him an advantage knowing what the future would, be but for that insight, he had to pay.

Lawrence went slow and cautious until he had to stop because he came to a dead end and was lost. The forest looked unfamiliar. The trees were gnarled and stunted. On each side of the wagon, as far as the eye could see, there was a large bog. And he couldn't turn the carriage around or else he would end up getting stuck in the dark-brown water that looked similar to the color of strong tea.

It was a prehistoric landscape with peat and moss islands growing in abundance among bare-skinned alders, crimson petal dogwoods, blueberries, and cranberries. In front of them, blocking their way, as the trail ended, were tall eighty-foot black spruce and tamarack trees. The tamarack trees with their fine needles gave the forest a filmy dreamlike appearance. They were the two types of plants that dominated the edges of the bog.

The bright yellow and crimson leaves burned into his eyes while he looked around for a way out, but there was none. He knew that eventually he would have to wake up Daniel and Abigail and tell them they were lost. But in the meantime, he got down from the buckboard and looked out at the expanse of forest which made him panicky.

He could smell the skunk cabbage and the rotting vegetation. At his feet, a northern pitcher plant caught his eye. It was trapping insects inside a large modified oval fleshy petal. Inside the greenish-purplish leaves, the downward pointing hairs prevented the insects from crawling out once they were trapped inside. Flies and beetles struggled valiantly by flapping their wings and stroking with their legs against the hairs of the oval green cul-de-sac. Lawrence could hear the buzzing of their wings as they tried to get out of the deathtrap. But they fell down into the swamp in the bottom of the carnivorous plant. They would swim for as long as they could and then would succumb to exhaustion. And eventually, the plant would digest them.

"Wake up, everybody," Lawrence shouted. Then he went over to the horse and unhitched him from the carriage.

"What's going on, Lawrence?" Abigail asked. "Are we near home yet?" She stretched and looked around. "This place doesn't look familiar."

"Dis is not a good place. We has to get out of here, Mista' Lawrence," Daniel said. Something in the back of Daniel's mind told him to get some matches. He went to the back of the carriage and buried his black paw inside one of the large duffel bags and pulled out a handful of matches and stuck them in his front pocket.

"That's what we're going to do if I have anything to say about it." With that, Lawrence brought Rebel to the back of the carriage. "Abby, come over here and hold the horse while me and Daniel turn the wagon around."

In the meanwhile, the rain became heavier and heavier until it was torrential. Before they could begin to turn the wagon, the swamp began to fill up and overflow its banks and cover the wheels.

"Get Rebel out of here, Abby," Lawrence hollered through the downpour. The noise of the heavy rain hitting the carriage made it difficult for them to talk to each other. Their soaked clothes hung on their bodies like wet sacks. Abigail pulled Rebel by the mouth to higher ground and stood there under a tamarack tree for protection.

"I swear I won't let this rain get the best of me!" Lawrence shouted and then took off his hat and slapped it on the seat of the carriage. "Come on, Daniel, help me push this wagon out of the mud." Lawrence rested his chest against the front wheel and grabbed the spokes as he pressed hard against them, tugging, slipping, and pushing his cheek against the metal of the wheel, until he slipped through the muck. While this was all being done, he looked up to the sky and shouted, "Damn you to hell, God. What have I done to deserve this?"

The two men grunted and groaned, trying to turn the carriage so it faced back out of the bog, but it was too heavy and they were too weak. They only managed to get the wagon turned halfway so that the back wheels and the front wheels sat firmly in the swamp.

"I don't think God's going to help us, Mista' Lawrence," Daniel said. "Weez better find some place dat's dry and comfortable." Their faces, their boots and shoes, their overalls, and their hands were covered in mud.

"I think you're right, Daniel. You and Abigail are drenched. I'm sorry that I got you into this." The raindrops stung his face, and the thunder rattled the marshy ground at his feet, the lighting flashed across the sky. In and among all this chaos, Lawrence went into a rage, pulling out his pistol and pointing it at the sky. He shot all the bullets through the pouring rain, screaming all the while, seeing in his mind's eye the bullets piercing the chest of what he imagined was God. The purple smoke from the gun lingered around the carriage. Lawrence exhausted, slumped over the lifeless wagon and sobbed.

Daniel walked over to Lawrence, putting his hand on his shoulder. "Mista' Lawrence, I think we better find some place to get in out of the rain. We can fight with God later."

Lawrence picked up his head and looked over his arm at Daniel. He marveled at Daniel's dispassionate, logical assessment of their situation. *How could I think that this little black man was a dumb brute?* he thought.

"You're right," Lawrence said. "Let's get out of here, friend."

The two men walked over to Abigail. She had been attending to the horse all this time under a tree. Her hair clung to the sides of her skull and her bonnet sagged on top of her head, and she was pulling up her shoulders and scrunching her chin in her neck. The horse's tint had changed because he was so wet that his coat took on a shiny coppery color. He dropped his head close to his hoofs and pulled down his ears close to his head in anger.

"While I was standing here, I saw a cave close to the edge of the swamp," Abigail said. She pulled Rebel along stepping knee-deep into the bog. Lawrence and Daniel followed close behind. The two men leaned into the horse for support while they sloshed through the quagmire.

All of a sudden, Daniel started to sing, soft at first and then louder as they approached the cave.

> Way down upon the Swanee River,
> Far, far away
> That's where my heart is turning ever
> That's where the old folks stay
> All up and down the whole creation,
> Sadly I roam
> Still longing for the old plantation
> And for the old folks at home.

Then he stopped singing, seeming to forget the lyrics. "Oh yeah. I remember now," he said. But he only sang what he could recall and what seemed appropriate at the time.

All the world is sad and dreary everywhere I roam
Oh lord, how my heart grows weary
Far from the old folks at home
One little hut among the bushes
One that I love
When shall I see the bees a humming,
All 'round the comb
When shall I hear the banjo strumming,
Down by my good old home.

"That was nice, Daniel," Abigail said.

"I is just happy to be going some place that's dry."

"Here it is," Abigail said. Then they splashed out of the swamp and into a cave that everybody could stand up in, even the horse was protected from the rain. He stamped his foot and sneezed and shook off the rain. The cavity looked like the mountain had opened up its welcoming mouth to let the travelers relax inside of it. They lounged on the lush green moss inside of the grotto.

"Want me to start a fire?" Daniel asked. He reached into his pocket and pulled out two parlor matches. He struck one on a dry rock. Then he reached around and gathered up kindling to make a blaze. After a while, he had a raging inferno going, and they all huddled around it, warming the palms of their hands and then blowing into them and rubbing them together.

While they sat there staring into the fire, Lawrence not particularly talking to anyone but more to himself asked the question, "How can I pray to God, not to let me be mad?"

Daniel answered the question as if Lawrence was asking him. "You don't have to pray to God, Mista' Lawrence." He poked a branch into the middle of the fire. "You won't go mad, just gotz ta know dat the world don't make any sense."

Lawrence looked deep and hard into the fire, and there was silence for a couple of minutes, then he said, "You're right again, Daniel. I should've realized that. Everything I saw in the war should have convinced me that the world is out of joint, and that men's minds don't know what the truth is."

"We ain't special. We're just lucky or unlucky. We're just in the right place or the wrong place. We're just born too early or born too late," Daniel said.

"If I could believe that I think my life would be easier," Lawrence said, looking at Daniel and then staring into the fire. "If I could only get this bug out of my brain, if I could only make it stop buzzing, if I could only squish it under my foot, everything would be all right."

Daniel suddenly got up and started to walk out the cave entrance.

"Where are you going, Daniel?" Lawrence asked.

"I'm a going to get one of the duffel bags sozs we can have somethin' to eat."

"I should be the one that's going," Lawrence said.

"I don't mind, Mista' Lawrence. I'll be right back."

Ten minutes after Daniel had returned, they were all sitting around the fire with pointed sticks suspended over the flames roasting red beef. "Boy, these are a far cry from those Delmonico steaks we had in New York, aren't they, Abby?" Lawrence asked with a tight-lipped smile coming across his face.

"Oh, I don't know," she said as she put the stick close to her mouth and bit off a piece. "To me, it tastes even better. It's as if we're the only people in the world, and we go out and kill for supper."

They stayed protected and warm in the cave for the rest of the night. Come morning, the rain had stopped, and the sun was sending shafts of light through the swamp. The damp cold air of the morning and the warmth of the sun made a foggy mist form on the surface of the bog.

"Come on, let's get out of here," Lawrence said. "Let's hook Rebel back onto the carriage so we can pull it around and face it in the right direction." His elbows pointed up as he rested his fists on his hips, and he leaned forward. He was ready to go.

They hooked the horse onto the carriage and Lawrence and Daniel rocked the wagon out of the mud while Abigail pulled at Rebel. Finally, the cart had been turned around and was facing in the right direction. "Nowz maybe we can go home," Daniel said, letting out a long sigh of relief.

They were now all back in the coach. "I'm not absolutely sure what direction we should take," Lawrence said. He threw up his hands, palms open. They had come to two paths that went north but in what direction that they need to go was a mystery.

"Let's travel north along the stonewalls that we see. Those are always a good indication of the farm being nearby," Abigail said. She pointed up the road.

"That's a good idea, Abby, you can be the navigator on my boat any time," Lawrence said and then kissed her on the cheek. Then he snapped the carriage whip just above the ear of the horse and they were off.

While they traveled back home, Lawrence stared at the mountains. The peaks squeezed them in from both sides. They were high for New England, a hundred feet, and the sun was glinting off their bald tops, possibly reflecting deposits of fool's gold.

It brought to mind Mount Olympus, where the gods lived. He imagined them reclining on their royal beds, lifting up their goblets into the air and making a toast as they drank the ambrosia from the classes, and laughed at the actions of the puny mortals on the earth below them.

And he wondered if it were true about what he and Abigail had read—that they were keeping an eye on the mortals below, that they were moving them around like pieces on a chessboard.

"They build their walls around here just like Pa does," Abigail said.

"Yeah, but they don't have a Union soldier buried under 'em like we do." Lawrence turned away and looked down at the wagon wheel, trying to understand why he brought up the subject of Burton and regretting he had ever said it.

"Why did you have to say that, Lawrence? I had almost forgotten." Instead of looking at the stonewalls to mark their way home, Abigail turned her back to them and scrunched close into Lawrence's side.

"Miss Abigail. Sometimes good tings come out of evil," Daniel said from the back of the carriage. He grabbed hold of the front seat, pulling himself closer to the couple. "Doze walls are beautiful. They is like the pyramids dat the Egyptians built in the Bible. They buried their kings under them."

"I'm sorry, Abby, I wasn't thinking," Lawrence said. "I meant it as a joke, but I realize it's not funny." He was anxious to get back home so he snapped the reins three times hard and fast on Rebel's rump. The horse stole a fast glance back over his shoulder and then trotted faster up the trail.

Lawrence knew they were going in the right direction because the sun was at his back, just over his right shoulder. The same trees he had seen on the shore were smaller and stunted the farther north he went. A small acorn of hope and peace started to grow in his gut. And the closer he got to home, the bigger the acorn grew.

After an hour of travel, Abigail sat up quickly and pointed her finger. "Look, look. Isn't that Mr. Martin's pond? Sure it is. I know that old rowboat and worn-out dock anywhere."

"You're right, Abby, that's the place," Lawrence shouted. As children, they had always used the pond as a swimming hole. It was only a couple of miles away from the farm.

Before Lawrence could stop the wagon, Abigail jumped off and ran toward the pond. She sprinted by a stand of long cattails which startled a blue heron. The grey bird with the long neck squeaked and immediately flapped its long powerful wings, catapulting it skyward.

Then she darted through a patch of blue flag iris. Their tiny blue petals bent and bowed to the young lady as she stripped off her clothes, followed by her splashing into the water.

Lawrence wasn't going to miss out going for a dip in their old swimming hole. "Daniel, watch the horse. I'm going for a swim," Lawrence said as he handed him the reins and then jumped off the wagon and headed in the direction where he had last seen Abigail. He hopped while he pushed the underbrush aside the best way he could as he made his way to the water.

He finally got to the moss-covered bank where Abigail had discarded her clothes. They were at random, draped on nearby blueberry bushes, and hung on the branches of a white paper birch. He started to fold his clothes neatly, and finally, in frustration, he said to himself, "Oh, the hell with it." He tore off his clothes and jumped into the millpond.

Lawrence dove in like a bullet from a rifle. The bubbles followed him through to the bottom of the pond. He kicked his feet and spun in the water like a dolphin and thought back to when he was a boy and how he loved to swim. Here, in this water, he was free and mobile. He could move quickly through the thick pond water, not like on land where he had to hobble along. He dove down to the bottom among the stalks of the white lily pad plants. His toes squished into the bottom of the swimming hole, and he pushed off with all his might so that he broke through the surface of the water.

Abigail was already on top floating and waiting for Lawrence to appear. "This is grand, isn't it, Lawrence?" She splashed water in his face and laughed.

"I feel like a boy again," he said. At once, he swam over to Abigail and took her in his arms. He could feel her breasts on his chest, and her young strong body balanced in his arms. They kissed, and as they did, they sunk back down into the water. They smiled at each other beneath the crystal clear liquid and kissed again and held each other's hands as they twirled around.

Finally, they breached the surface like two young whales, gasping for air and then swam toward the shore. They both lay there naked as the afternoon sun warmed their wet skin.

"Lawrence, you swim like a fish," Abigail said with a broad smile, and the muscles around her eyes contracting as she turned her head to face him.

"I sure would like to be a fish, floating, swimming, and just living." He got up and shook as a cold shiver went up his spine while he put his clothes back on. Looking down at Abigail, he said, "You better get dressed so we can go home." The rotting smell of the bog was gone now, replaced by the sweet aroma of the clean pool.

"Okay," she said, and at the same time, snatched at her clothes hanging on the bushes.

While Abigail got dressed, Lawrence couldn't help thinking that she was like some kind of woodland sprite whose home was in the center of the pond, and that if he touched her, she would dissolve into the air.

When they finally got back to the carriage, Lawrence held onto the reins even tighter now because he realized that Rebel also knew that he was close to his place of birth. His nostrils flared, and he could smell the familiar grass and trees that were near his home. He also saw the pond, and he remembered being ridden to it many times in the past. He was hopeful that all his senses were telling him the truth so he quickened his pace and galloped toward the scent of his native soil.

They came through a back road that led into the farm. They passed the fields of corn, potatoes, and tomatoes, until finally they pulled up next to the big red barn. At that very moment, Noah came out of the summer kitchen and ran over to the wagon.

"My prodigal children have come back home," he said as Abigail got down off the wagon and hugged him. He squeezed her hard and growled with contentment.

"We're so glad to be home, Pa," Abigail said.

Then Lawrence got down off his seat and all at once flopped on all fours on the ground and kissed it.

With Abigail still in his arms hugging him, Noah said, "What in the tarnation are you doing, son?"

"I was so happy to be home I had to kiss the ground," he said, looking up at Noah.

Everybody laughed, making that incident the link in the chain that pulled them back into the farm life.

"Come on in the house and relax," Noah said.

The summer kitchen was like the hub in a wheel. It was the center of all the activity in the farm, more than any other room in the house. They all ended up sitting around the informal pine table drinking their coffee, talking about their adventures in New York, and telling Pa how happy they were to be home. Lawrence sat on the chair with Abigail hugging him and sitting on his lap. Daniel had the chair turned around and was straddling it and resting his forearms on the back support of the seat. Noah sat leaning forward with his elbows on the table and the coffee cup in his hands waiting for the details of the married couple's adventure.

Lawrence could see that Noah was happy to have his family back home again. "No work today. It's a holiday. Just smell the farm again," he said. Then he got up. "I've got some work to do." He went through the door and disappeared into the fields.

Lawrence at first was baffled by what Noah uttered. Smell the farm? What did he mean? But as he got up and put his coffee cup in the Zink sink, he understood what Noah had said—the sharp metal smell of the sink, the food covered aroma of the cast iron stove, the homemade nutty bouquet of the coffee brewed on the stove top, the natural scent of the pine table and chairs, the smell of the earthy soil wafting through the open window. Even the odor of the cow manure, at once offensive and then sweet, made him smile and appreciate what Noah said as he left the kitchen.

After that, Abigail went into the sitting room to rock on the rocking chair and look at the brochures that they had brought back from New York.

Lawrence went to the barn to see to Rebel and make sure that he was settled and had enough hay. Daniel disappeared into the fields just as Noah had done.

Now, it was common things that he dealt with every day that brought back the demons of war to his mind. Lawrence scooped up a can full of oats which smelled like molasses and put it in Rebel's trough. And as he did, a pitchfork of an old memory pierced his mind. He wasn't sure if it was the smell, the sound, or the very presence of the beast, but his mind went back to images of bloated dead horses, lining the sides of the road as he traveled.

He tried to push the memory out of his mind. In desperation, he went over to the old still, got a glass canning jar, and filled the glass from the ten-gallon milk can which had been turned into a still. It was even warm and packed a punch. "Ah," he said as he drank it down, filling up the glass jar three times more and drinking every last drop. The memory started to fade away so he drank some more and some more, until he had forgotten just how much he had drank. He tumbled back onto a bale of hay becoming unconscious.

23

BULLETS AGAINST THE DEVILS

LAWRENCE SUDDENLY WOKE up, and looking around, he thought that he had died and gone to heaven. There were flowers everywhere he looked; purple iris were hung all along the top of the room and the lighter-colored violets were in clumps and placed on the dressers; large yellow sunflowers were attached to the back of the headboard, and red and yellow carnations were placed next to the wash basin. "Wha…What's going on?" Lawrence shouted.

"Daniel and me carried you from the barn and put you in the bed," Abigail said.

"Thanks, Abby," he said, blinking his eyes and looking around the room.

"Pa, put all these flowers in the room as a celebration for our new marriage," she said as she pulled a carnation up to her nose and took a big whiff.

"Yeah, real nice," Lawrence said. "I've got to go for a walk, Abby." Lawrence had to get out of the room because he felt closed in as if he were in a casket with flowers all around him.

By the time Lawrence had woken up from his drunken stupor, it was nine o'clock and the sky was dark. He was shaky as he staggered down the stairs, grabbed his cane, and went out the door of the summer kitchen. When he was out in the field, he found the cart that he used for picking the vegetables and lay down on it looking up at the stars. The night sky was an inky blackness dotted with twinkling silver stars.

The sky in early September of the year was in transition, possibly mimicking Lawrence's life. The summer triangle pointed to the Celestial Sea, with the constellations Capricorn, the sea goat; and off to the West Aquarius, the water bearer; and Pisces, the fish. These constellations showed a pool of blackness between them, much like the feelings inside his gut.

Although being out in the field alone, with his mind in the sky, between the stars turned out to be soothing. The squeak of the field crickets and the croaking of the pond frogs gave his mind a rest from the human world. He could swear that he felt the turning of the earth below him, and it seemed to heal his insides and put at bay the devils in his brain. He spent the whole night staring up at the stars.

In the morning, Abigail was standing over him. "Lawrence, Lawrence, wake up," she shouted.

"Oh, sorry about this, Abigail. I just felt comfortable out here," he said as he negotiated himself off the cart and onto his cane.

"Are you acting like this because of the things you saw in the war?"

"Yes. The simple fact is that witnessing killing and destruction doesn't make me feel like a hero. It just makes me feel like a victim. These things in my head pull me in every direction, and I have to find a way to kill them." Lawrence walked away and then turned back suddenly. "Do you understand what I'm telling you?"

"No, I don't. All I understand is that I'm getting frustrated, and I can't live like this anymore."

"I know what you're feeling, Abby. I live with frustration every minute of the day," he said. "All I can tell you is that I won't give up on us or myself." Then he walked away and didn't see Abigail for the rest of the day.

He was still feeling pulled in the direction of his illness, but he was determined to fight this unseen enemy so he went over to the stream, kneeled down, and splashed his face with the cold clean water. He gasped because the crystal clear liquid was so cold. "Ah. That's a miracle," he said to himself. The water made him feel alive, but more important than that was that it jolted him back into the present.

"What's that?" he whispered to himself. Within arm's length was a brownish-black crystal rock, resembling an irregular egg. When he picked it out of the water, he noticed that it had a smooth surface and seemed heavy for such a small stone. Then he realized that it was a lodestone. He put it in his pocket and forgot about it.

Later that day, while he was in the cornfield with Daniel, he showed him the stone. "Daniel, come over here for a second," he yelled. "Do you know what this rock is?"

"Lem me see, Mista' Lawrence." He cautiously walked over, staring all the while at what was in Lawrence's open hand. "Why that's the healing stone. They sez it fixes whatever ails ya."

"How's that, Daniel?" Lawrence asked. Lawrence knew it was superstition, but he was willing to listen to Daniel's folktale. *Maybe there's some truth in it*, he thought.

"Well, when I was a boy in South Carolina, my sister got mighty sick. No matter what my mama tried, it didn't help." Daniel had a far-off look in his eyes.

"Yeah, so what did she do?" Lawrence asked.

"She told us be good and look after my sister whilz she took a ride on our mule in the woods. When she come back, a day later, she had a poltis in one bag and those stones in da other."

"Yeah, yeah," Lawrence said, getting impatient.

"She puts the poltis on my sister's belly, and the stones on her chest and her head."

"And what happened?" Lawrence asked.

"The next day, she wasa laughin' and eatin' up a storm," he said. "They is powerful magic, Mista' Lawrence."

"Where'd she get that stuff from?" Lawrence asked.

"It was from Mother Cleo. She's a medicine lady, lives in the woods. I been there once. She has skinned lizards, frogs and snakes all over her shack and has bobcats and cougars for pets."

"How does it work?" Lawrence asked, looking at it in his hand.

"You rubs it and puts it on the place where it hurts," Daniel said.

"Thanks, Daniel. You can go back to work now." When Daniel left and was out of sight, Lawrence took out his knife and scraped the stone. To him, it didn't seem like anything special until his knife stuck to the rock. It was magnetic. From that day on, Lawrence used the stone the way Daniel suggested. He rubbed it on his temples when he felt the demons coming on and he rubbed it on his chest when he couldn't catch his breath.

For some unexplained reason, the magnetite stone worked. It seemed to lessen Lawrence's attacks. Whether it was just his belief in the stone or the fact that it actually succeeded didn't matter to Lawrence because for some unexplained reason, it brought him some relief. He scraped down the surface to make it smooth and kept it deep down in his pocket so he wouldn't lose it. Lawrence was gathering up an arsenal of weapons that he could use to combat this evil spirit in his head.

He sat on his little cart, content for the moment, in and among the cornstalks, feeling that he was protected and hidden away from the real world, but that feeling was about to crumble around him. He could hardly believe his eyes. It was John Webb leading his horse through the field of corn. John stopped and looked down at Lawrence.

Lawrence looked up into the face of evil. "What are you doing here, I thought we got rid of you?" Lawrence said as he got up to face him.

"I'm not that easy to get rid of," John said.

"Aren't you afraid of Noah? He said he'd kill you the next time he saw you."

"He's just a farmer. What can he do to hurt me?" John asked while taking off his hat and putting it on the pommel of the saddle. Then he pulled the farm cart over and sat on it.

"Plenty, if he finds you on his land," Lawrence said.

He whipped at the cornstalks with his riding crop while he talked. "I'll tell you what I'll do. I'll have my men pick for you, still give me my quota and you can keep the illusion that you're still doing your job, and nobody will be the wiser."

"But I'll know what the truth is. I can't live with myself under those circumstances," Lawrence said. Trying to calm down, Lawrence put his hand in his pocket and rubbed the magic stone, but in this situation, it didn't work.

"Do you want your pretty wife and Noah to be in the middle of this? It's better if it's between you and me," John said.

Lawrence's anger exploded. He jumped on John and snatched his riding crop from his hand and then pressed it against his throat trying to choke him. The cornstalks snapped and the horse backed up as the two men rolled on the ground. All of a sudden, Lawrence felt somebody grab him under his arms and then stand him up. John's men held Lawrence tight. John picked up his riding crop and slashed Lawrence across the face with it.

"Okay…okay, you win. I'll do what you want, just don't get anybody else involved in our bargain," Lawrence said. "I still have to tell Daniel about this."

"Whatever you have to do to keep this little agreement going is up to you. Keep him in line," John Webb said. "We'll find you at dusk so nobody sees what's going on."

"All right," Lawrence said. The two men released him and then they all slithered back into the woods.

Lawrence hobbled through the field about a half mile to where Daniel was working. He walked up behind him and put his hand on his shoulder. "Daniel, we've got to talk."

"Yes, Mista' Lawrence, what is it?" He turned and faced him.

"Well, you remember those men we met that wanted to sell you and all the trouble we had with them. Well, they're back. And I struck up a deal with them so that Abigail and Noah wouldn't get involved. You just have to do what I tell you and don't let Noah know about what's happening. I feel like a slave but what can I do. Do I have your word that you'll keep this between us?"

"I know all 'bout bein' a slave. I was a slave once. Dis is even worse than that. But if we has to give up ourselves to keep Noah and Abigail safe then yo' has my word," Daniel said.

"Thanks, Daniel. We can handle this together. You're a good man," Lawrence said. Then he shook his hand. "Do you hear somebody talking? I hear the voice of my captain barking orders at me. Don't you hear that?"

"No, Mista' Lawrence, I don't hear nothing," Daniel said. "Are you having one of your attacks again? Wait right here, I'll be back." A minute later, Daniel returned with a handful of green plants. He handed them to Lawrence. "Smell dis' mint, Mista' Lawrence."

Lawrence did as he was told and the voices faded away. "Wow! That really worked. I can't hear my dead captain's orders anymore."

"Chew a couple of pieces," Daniel said. "Dat helps too."

He picked the small green plant from his hand and popped it in his mouth. It tasted bitter as he chewed it, and when he breathed it in, it was cold in his mouth. *I've found another thing that will help me do battle with my demons*, he thought. He quickly put it in his pocket next to the stone. Now the soldier had two bullets to fire at the fiends that lived in his head.

"I think I hear the buckboard coming, Daniel," Lawrence said. "I hope its Abigail. I'm hungry."

"I hopes so. I'm powerful hungry too," Daniel said.

By now, it was five or six and the sun was low, peaking through the trees. Dusk would be descending on the farm very soon.

The old buckboard squeaked and rattled coming up the road. Abigail pulled up in front of Daniel and Lawrence. "Whoa," she said. Then she got down from the carriage and put leather ankle ties on Rebel's legs so he couldn't run away. She walked over to the two men with a big wicker picnic basket in her hand. "Here, boys, I made some sandwiches."

Lawrence bent forward and kissed Abigail on the cheek. "Thank you, honey. We were dying of hunger." He noticed that she was wearing the snake necklace and the Florentine earrings that he bought her in New York, but he was too hungry to mention it.

Daniel and him opened up the top of the basket and grabbed the sandwiches like two young lions pouncing on their prey. There were peppermint candies, and like two children, the men grabbed a handful of each and put them in their pockets. Lawrence was happy to see Abigail and to know that she had brought them food, but in the back of his mind, he knew that John Webb and his men would be arriving any minute.

"I wore the jewelry that you bought me. Aren't they beautiful?" She put her fingers under her earlobe and pushed them out so the boys could get a better look at them.

"Yes, I noticed," Lawrence said, glancing quickly at her ear.

"Why didn't you sleep in our bed last night, Lawrence?" Abigail asked. "I missed you."

"I'm sorry, Abby. When I sleep in a bed, I feel like I'm in a coffin. I have to get out."

"Why don't you just calm down. Then everything would be all right," Abigail said. "If you just relax, you would be all right."

"Don't you think the first thing I want is to be calm?" Her naive solution made him mad and feel alone. He threw his half-eaten sandwich into the nearby woods. "But it's the last thing I can be."

"What's the matter, don't you like the sandwich I made for you?" Abigail asked, watching the sandwich spread apart into pieces as it was thrown into the forest.

"I lost my appetite," Lawrence said.

He reached into the picnic basket and pulled out a glass canning jar that still had the top on it. He pulled off the top and drank the beer inside. It was called "flip," and was composed of beer, rum, and sugar.

"I made that flip beer especially for you and Daniel. I thought you would both like it. I thought the beer would be good for you. It would calm you down."

"I told you, Abby, it's got nothing to do with being calm," Lawrence said a little bit louder.

"Okay, Lawrence, don't get mad, I just want to try…I just wanted to understand," she said. "I also made peppermint cakes and your favorite mince pie. There's also some peppermint candies in there for both of you."

"Yeah, yeah…Okay that's fine," he said. He guzzled down the beer and looked over the hill, expecting John Webb and his band of thieves to appear any second.

"It's all in your head, Lawrence," Abigail said with a smile. "Can't we talk about what you're thinking? Maybe then we can figure out what to do."

"Of course, it's in my head. Where else would it be?" Knowing that it's in there doesn't make it any easier." With that in mind, he lashed out at the corn plants with his hands and feet. He pulled out some plants by their roots and flung them into the air and stepped on others until they were flat on the ground. All of a sudden, he stopped and began to pant.

Daniel stood like a statue not knowing what to say or do. Then he said, "I's goin' to tend to the horse." He left without looking back.

Lawrence walked over to Abigail, put his face right next to hers, and put his hands around her neck. "I could snap your neck like a twig," he said.

Abigail pushed Lawrence away and crying, ran through the field to the carriage. When she got there, she directed Daniel to take the ankle bracelets off Rebel. "I'm going back to the house," she said. Abigail whipped the horse, and at the same time, turned the animal back toward the house.

As Lawrence watched her leave, he regretted what he had done, but it was as if he was being pushed from behind, sliding down a steep hill with no way to stop. The feeling was acid in his blood. It welled up deep in his belly and traveled through his chest, exploding behind his eyes, and before he knew it, into his hands. He was only aware of what he had done after Abigail shoved him in the chest.

24

ABIGAIL MEETS
JOHN WEBB AGAIN

ABIGAIL FELT BETRAYED and abused, because after all, all she wanted to do was understand how Lawrence felt and what she could do to help. She snapped the buggy whip above Rebel's ear, and poor Rebel wanting to please her, trotted as fast as he could. She could hardly see the road through her tears. Then out of the woods came John Webb.

He grabbed the reins of the horse and pulled the carriage to a stop.

"John, what are you doing here, I thought you left forever?" Abigail asked. "You should leave before Pa sees you. He'll shoot you on sight."

"I'll take that chance. I want to see you again, Abigail," he said. "Madam, please get down off the carriage and talk to me."

Abigail could feel her face and neck get warm. She wanted to hide her embarrassment so she looked down at the road. He is a gentleman. *He has courted many women and for him to want to see me again makes me feel important,* she thought.

Abigail was torn inside between getting down or whipping Rebel so that she could get by. She sat there for a while looking at him and deciding what to do. But John made the decision for her. He got down off his horse, walked over to the carriage, and lifted her off the seat, putting her on the ground in front of him.

"There, now you have to talk to me." He took off his hat and bowed to her.

"What do you want? I have to be going," she said as she folded her arms in front of her chest, looking down at him.

"Oh, give a tired soldier a break," he said, turning his head to the side and then looking up at her with a false half smile.

Abigail laughed, unfolded her arms, and sat on a nearby rock. The earrings were becoming heavy on her earlobes, like two anvils pulling her ears down. She wanted to get rid of them so she took them off and placed them on the rock.

"Okay, soldier, I'm here. Talk." She stretched out her legs, folded her hands in her lap, and tilted her head, waiting for her little soldier to speak. She felt like a queen admonishing one of her knights for not being as attentive as he might.

John stood over her and then put his foot on the rock that she was sitting on so that he could be closer to her. He leaned in resting his elbow on his knee getting close to her face. "I don't think people understand who I am, Abigail. True, I am a gentleman, but I'm also a soldier." He rested his hand on his saber and longingly looked down the road. "I'm alone now. My ties to the plantation in Kentucky are cut off. I have to survive."

As Abigail listened to his story, she came to the conclusion that John Webb wasn't a devil or an enemy to be despised; he was just a lonely displaced soldier looking for a home. More and more, she came to admire this stranger and to see Lawrence as a coward. *After all*, she thought, *Charlie Jillson, one of his army buddies, even with no left arm, was doing better than Lawrence.* This John Webb seemed to be branded unfairly as a scoundrel.

After listening to him, she felt that she could take John into her confidence. "Being a soldier, can you tell me something," she asked.

"Yes, what do you want to know?" He said.

"Lawrence has been acting strangely. And I don't know what to make of it. He scares me sometimes, and I don't know what to do about it," she said.

"He probably was remembering back to all the punishments he had to go through. Maybe when he was in the army, he 'talked back,' or left his post without a pass, or refused to salute," he said. "He may have been punished with a loaded knapsack of bricks, or ridden a wooden horse." Abigail could see him recalling the incidents as he looked up at the sky. "We had a platform put up between twenty-five and thirty feet high, and we put the soldier up there all day isolated away from everyone else as a punishment," he said.

"Do you think that's why he acts the way he does?" Abigail asked.

"Could be," John said. "We had a lot of soldiers on sick call all the time. One boy refused to eat and became skin and bones. We had to discharge him. I sometimes wonder if that soldier was faking."

The memory of Lawrence when he first came back from the army popped into her head. *Could that be why Lawrence looked so skinny when he came back? Was he faking it?* she thought.

"Do you think he was punished when he was in the army?" Abigail asked.

"Could be. Or maybe he just wasn't a very good soldier," John said.

"I'm living on pins and needles. Every time I see him, I don't know what to expect," Abigail said while getting up and walking over to the carriage, about to get up on the seat again. John held her hand as she stepped up and then sat.

Looking up at her, he said, "I don't want to worry you anymore because I think this meeting between us made us friends. But Lawrence can do whatever he wants to you. He can even beat you, and the law would look the other way."

"How do you know that, John?" she asked.

"I don't know the laws up here, but in Kentucky, the man is in control. I'd be careful if I were you," he said.

"I can't talk to Pa about this. He wouldn't understand," Abigail said, looking out toward the farmhouse with a blank stare.

"You can talk to me," John said. Then he picked up her hand and kissed it.

Abigail smiled at him. "Okay, when?" It was a hollow promise because it would take more courage to see him than she had, or so she thought.

"Tomorrow. At that old stone wall over there at dusk," he said, pointing at the stone wall in the north pasture.

Abigail didn't say a word but inside she was churning with anxiety. She hesitated going back to the farmhouse but where else could she go. She slowly shook her head in disgust and looked at John for an answer. Just as she picked up the reins to leave, John stepped in front of the carriage and held on to the horse's bridle.

"What are you doing, John? I have to be going," she said.

"Will I see you again like you promised?" he asked.

"I don't think we should ever see each other again."

"Why, are you afraid of your husband?"

"A little."

"A little or a lot?" John grabbed the carriage and pulled himself closer to Abigail.

"A lot." She had a dry mouth and sweaty palms. For the first time, she realized that she really was afraid of her husband. She snapped the whip above the horse's ear, and Rebel was off. John jumped away from the carriage and onto the ground just in time. She glanced back over her right shoulder and saw John Webb standing in the dust, staring at her as she left.

All of a sudden halfway down the road, she became conscious of the fact that she had left her earrings on the rock that she was sitting on. There was a time when she would have rushed back, scared that her precious gift had been stolen or that she had lost them forever, but those days were gone. She just kept on going and snapped the whip twice, making Rebel go faster. In her imagination, she saw the earrings melting into the stone and disappearing.

Even the close fitting snake-like necklace became heavy around her neck, and it felt like it was a noose strangling her. She held the reins with one hand and grabbed the necklace with the other, jerking it off and flinging it onto the filthy road. And as she did that, some of the pieces broke off and clattered on the seat.

After that, she began to cry again, but this time, it was different. It became an angry sobbing. *Who does Lawrence think he is treating me that way?* she thought. As a result, she took her anger out on Rebel, snapping the reins harder and lashing the whip into the air until the horse was running full speed.

Finally, she reached the barn, pulling Rebel to a stop while the dust followed behind her, catching up to the wagon, covering it in a cloud of gray powder as the carriage came to a skidding stop. She jumped off the seat and ran into the house directly in front of Noah. Noah grabbed Rebel, and with a puzzled look on his face, watched Abigail streak by.

Rebel, white lather sticking to his sides after the run, panted hard through his nostrils and pawed the ground.

After Noah had stabled Rebel, Abigail heard him coming up the stairs. She was in her bed crying into her pillow. "Abigail, you all right?" he asked as he walked down the hall.

"No, Pa," she said while holding tight to her pillow. Then she sat up on the edge of the bed cradling the pillow against her stomach. Noah came into the room and sat in the chair next to the bed. "I have a baby in my belly, and I can't even tell Lawrence because he won't talk to me."

"Oh, Abby, I'm so happy for ya," he said. He got up, walked over, and kissed Abigail on the forehead. So lightly that it seemed to Abigail that Pa thought she was made out of spun glass. Then he went back and sat on the chair.

"I owe you everything, but most of all, I owe you obedience. You took me in and adopted me and treated me like your own daughter. You gave me an education, and I respect you for that. But Lawrence is my husband, and I guess I have to do what he tells me to do."

"You are my daughter in every way," Noah said. "If I could take you away from Lawrence, I'd do it."

Abigail stared at the wall and then suddenly turned toward Noah and asked, "Do you think that Lawrence is a coward?"

"No," he said. He leaned forward, resting his elbows on his knees and looked deep into Abigail's eyes.

"How can you say that. How can you be so sure?" she asked. She wanted desperately for Pa to give her something that she could believe.

"Bcuse I've talked to him about the war and all the battles. I've raised him like my own son. I know him."

"He talked to you but not to me?" she asked.

"Maybe he didn't want ta tell you about the awful things he saw. Maybe he wanted ta protect you from all that hurt," Noah said. "He's no coward, Abby."

"But I'm not as fragile as a porcelain doll. I won't break," she said. "He can tell me anything, but I feel there's some kind of wall between us."

It was enough for her father to give his opinion. And his beliefs for her were the final word. *He lives up to his name Noah*, she thought. He's captain of the farm, managing to steer it in the right direction. For her whole life, what Pa said and believed in moved the farm along, sustained it and nurtured it. Even though everything that Lawrence did made him out to be a coward, if Noah said he wasn't, then Abigail accepted it.

25

DEVIL ON A PALE HORSE

MEANWHILE, BACK IN the field, the darkness had covered John Webb's men working in the field. Lawrence and Daniel were right there beside them, stealing the produce, just like the thieves that they hated.

John Webb rode all the way through the cornfield with the torch held in his hand high above his head. Then he stopped in front of Lawrence and Daniel, got off his white horse and walked over to the two men. "Nice job, boys. Keep it up. This will be the last time we're doing this. We'll be heading down south tomorrow," John said. "Winter will be hitting New England pretty soon."

"Can't say as I'm unhappy to see you go," Lawrence said. He stopped and looked at John's face reflected by the light of the torch, flickering between light and dark. His hard angular features reminded him of the devil's face—arrogant and mocking.

"I can't say I blame you," John said. "But you'll be rid of us come next week. I don't mind telling you I can't wait to get back home to Kentucky."

Lawrence turned back into the field and continued with snapping off the ears of corn and putting them into the basket. "Good riddance," Lawrence said.

"Now is that any way to treat a guest?" John asked.

"You're not a guest. You're just like a boil on my neck that I can't get rid of."

"Evidently, your wife thinks I'm a guest. She gave me these to remember her by," he said as he reached into his pocket and pulled out Abigail's earrings.

Lawrence turned around fast and caught a glimpse of the earrings that were in John's hand. "Where did you get those?" Lawrence asked.

"I just told you. They were a gift."

Lawrence wanted to strangle John Webb so he started to run toward him, but he felt somebody grabbing his arms from behind. "No, Mista' Lawrence, he's not worth it," Daniel said, holding tight on to Lawrence's arms from behind.

"Okay, son. Here you go," John said. "I don't have any use for them anyway." Then he handed them over to Lawrence. Lawrence looked at them to make sure they weren't damaged and slipped them in his pocket.

After that, he turned away from John because he was seething inside and wanted nothing better than to strangle this devil. *But Daniel was right, it was better just biding our time*, Lawrence thought.

Then something happened that Lawrence never expected.

"Lawrence"—he had his back turned away from John—"Lawrence, how would you like to come to Kentucky with me?" John asked.

Lawrence turned at a snail's pace back toward John. It was as if he was captured in a gel, and it was difficult to turn because his insides were seething. He could hardly believe what he had just heard. "What did you say? Did I hear you right?" Lawrence asked.

"Yeah, you heard me right. I could use somebody like you down there to see over the darkies," John said. "I like your spunk. You got guts."

"And what about Daniel, can I bring him along?" Lawrence asked.

"No, I don't think so. Your boy there got too many rights given to him. He's too civilized," John said.

"Are you serious?" Lawrence asked. "Or is this one of your tricks?"

"We're both soldiers. I understand what you went through. These people don't have the slightest idea what the war was like, especially your wife. If you change your mind and want to come along, stick this peacock feather between the rocks in that new wall you guys just built in the north pasture. That'll let me know to pick you up on the road in front of the farmhouse. John pulled out the feather from his hat band and handed it to Lawrence.

"You've got to be kidding," Lawrence said as he threw the feather on the ground.

John Webb snickered when he saw what Lawrence did with the feather. Then he pulled a whistle from his pocket and blew into it three quick times. Lawrence's skin crawled each time he blew the whistle.

All his men gathered around him. "Well, boys, that's it. Pack up, we're leaving tomorrow," John said. Then he turned to Lawrence. "Remember what I said. Think about it. You'll live like a king down there."

There was the clatter of the wagon wheels and the shuffling of the men as they loaded up the last of their stolen goods into the back of the US supply wagon and left by the road that snaked through the back of the farm.

Lawrence watched the parade of men, some with mud-soaked trousers, most with full beards, some with their rifles slung over their shoulders, looking down at the ground as they left but all marching wearily away from the farm. It was a welcome sight for Lawrence.

Daniel crackled through the old corn plants. "Mista' Lawrence, I's going back to the house ta gets some sleep," he said.

"Okay, Daniel, see you the morning," Lawrence said as he looked up at the night sky, and at the same time, he reached into his pocket and rubbed the lodestone. His opium pills had run out long ago, and he had noticed that he had to fight his emotional ups and downs, the depression, body weakness, the shaky feelings, the exhaustion, and most of all, the nightmares. He couldn't help thinking that he was fighting a battle inside himself worse than any that he had seen during the war. *I fought the soldier's disease, and won*, he thought. I have to use these little tricks to appease my mind and that's all right, but what do I do about Abigail?

While lying on the little cart and looking up at the sky, a tear rolled down his cheek. It surprised him because inside he was numb. Soon he fell asleep. It was the only place he could find any peace.

After a restless sleep, he suddenly awoke. This was the usual way he slept, in fits and starts, so he accepted it as normal. But something was different this time. He turned and looked into the darkness. Abigail was standing there in the aisle of cornstalk naked. Her young firm body glistened in the moonlight. She slowly walked toward Lawrence and then lay down on the cart next to him.

"I want you to want me," she said as she inched closer to him.

"I do want you," he said.

Lawrence's heart beat hard against his chest, and he tried to speak. But more words would not come. Seeing her there like that brought images to his mind of Aphrodite, the same goddess that he had read about in the *Iliad*.

259

"You've changed my life and put life in my belly. I'm not the little girl that you used to know, Lawrence. I'm a woman now. You can't drag me along like you used to," she said, looking up into his eyes.

"You're pregnant?" he asked.

"Yes," she said.

He reached into his pocket. "What are these?" he asked. "John Webb said you gave them to him as a present." Then he threw the earrings at her crumpled dress.

"No, I lost them," she said.

"This is too much, Abigail," he said as he got up off the cart. "I'm having enough trouble just staying sane, let alone having to take care of you and a child."

"What are you saying?" Abigail asked. At once, she got up and went over and slipped on her clothes and picked up the earrings and put them in the pocket of her dress.

"Is the baby mine or is it John Webb's?" he asked.

"I just happened to see him on the road, that's all," Abigail shouted as she pulled off an ear of corn and threw it at Lawrence. He held up his arm and dropped down on one knee.

"I have to leave. I have to find out who this person is inside of me, the one that came back from the war. Not the one that went to war." At that instant, Lawrence felt like that little boy who was dropped off at the farm those many years ago, lost and alone.

"Will I ever see you again?" Abigail asked.

"I don't know," he said as he walked toward her. She backed up, keeping her distance from Lawrence.

She quickly turned and sprinted through the cornfield back toward the farmhouse. That would be one of the last times he ever saw her.

Lawrence looked at his little cart and next to it were the delicate black ostrich feathers that John Webb had given him. He bent down and picked them up and looked at them for a long time, wondering if he should put the feathers in the wall as a signal that he accepted John's offer. He slipped through the cornfield and onto the dirt road, limping all the way.

On the way to the wall, Lawrence thought to himself how ironic it was that John Webb wanted him to put a feather in the wall where Burton was buried. What was that saying? A feather in your cap for a job well done. He felt like the gods were looking down at him and laughing at his troubles, and that somehow, they had orchestrated the events that had just taken place.

When he got there, he took off some flat rocks from the top of the wall and sandwiched them together with the ostrich feathers between them so it stood up straight and tall. Then he took two round rocks and squeezed them up against the flat rocks. The signal monument was done. With this one gesture, he was hopeful that his life would change for the better.

He reached into his pocket and took out a small little amber-colored bottle with a cork on the top. He popped the top and stuck the bottle under his nose. He took a deep whiff, making his eyes water and his heart jump. "Ahh, that's better," he said. This was another of his bullets that was used to fight his demons. The woman he got it from guaranteed that the spirits of ammonia was a surefire way to get rid of evil spirits, demons, and spells. All Lawrence knew for sure was that it worked.

Now he was alone so he hobbled back to his cart in the cornfield and lay down on it, anticipating a night's sleep under the stars. It felt like home sitting there in the dark, listening to the croaking frogs from the nearby pond and the squeak of the field crickets.

This was one time when he didn't need any of those bullets in his pocket to keep away the demons; the peppermint candy, the small green mint leaves, biting into a little lemon, cold water on his face, a lodestone rubbed between his fingers, or the little bottle of ammonia.

He lay down looking into the darkness of the night while the stars became his friends, shining their light into his mind. Here in the fields looking up at the stars, his body little by little became light and airy as if it had forgotten that it was attached to the earth.

Before he knew it, the dew was waking him up the next morning. It clung to his shirt and eyelashes and dripped off the little cart. This morning would be different because he was leaving the farm and Abigail. He walked to a stand of poplar trees near the farmhouse, leaning up against one of the trees, watching Noah, Abigail, and Daniel get in the buckboard and ride off into the fields.

He waited a couple of more minutes to make sure that they were gone. He clumped through the summer kitchen with his hobnailed boots and went upstairs to the bedroom to gather his things. All the rest of the morning and into the afternoon, he sat in the woods cozying up to a small fire, waiting for John Webb and his men to come by.

All of a sudden, Noah was making preparations to plow the field that was near him. He quickly doused the fire, stood up, and hid himself behind the trees.

Noah started plowing the field with Rebel pulling, straining, and leaning forward through the dark rich soil. He had the reins draped over his shoulders and his work boots sunk deep into the dirt. "That ta boy. Ya got it now," he said. After making three plowed furrows in the field, he came to an abrupt halt. "Whoa," he said. "We've done enough for now. Let's rest, Rebel." After he stopped, he took the reins off his shoulders and wrapped them around the handles of the plow. The horse sneezed and stamped its foot, seeming to say that it was anxious to keep plowing. It swished away the flies from its flanks.

Abigail stood on the edge of the field watching her father. In front of her, she held a picnic basket. She seemed to be waiting for a lull in the plowing. She walked carefully over the furrows of dirt as her black buttoned-up shoes sunk deep into the soil. "Pa, come over here and get something to eat," she hollered.

The field stretched out as far as the eye could see, curving to the left and out of sight past the forest. Noah swayed from side to side, stepping in the open furrowed soil in order to get to the edge of the field. On each side of the pasture, the forest squeezed close to the edge of the plowed ground. Trees of poplar, oak, and elm stood like sentinels protecting the deep woods. It was as if they were daring Noah to domesticate their ground.

Lawrence stood close to the field but hid behind an oak tree so that he would not be seen. He blended into the forest, more animal than a man, eyes alert and aware of every movement. He had his haversack and bedroll slung over his left shoulder. He stood there looking at everything that was going on. It made Lawrence feel like a stranger, although the cowbell brought back fond memories.

Abigail was ringing the cowbell, and a minute later, Daniel came out of the woods and sat next to Abigail and Noah.

How many times I answered that cowbell, to get sandwiches and beer, Lawrence thought. It was one of the most welcome sounds on the farm except for Abigail's voice. *Where did the bond between me and Abigail go? Why wasn't our love strong enough to keep us from drifting apart?*

These thoughts came to him as he stared at the trio sitting under the shade of the trees next to the field.

The illness that he brought back from the war and the guilt they felt for killing Burton were the wedges that came between them. He knew that his sickness was one of the problems that kept them apart. But he was determined that if he couldn't cure these feelings, he would have to live with them. And he came to realize that the marriage would not last and that it was better for both of them that he wrestled with his ghosts alone.

He leaned forward to get a better look and the sound of his haversack scraped against the tree, sending a chill up his spine. But most of all, he was trying to peek at a scene that he knew well, searching for that feeling of comfortable belonging. Although he knew that that naive feeling, which he felt so long ago, could never be captured again.

These were people that are givers. I've turned into a person that is a taker. *My illness made me that way*, he thought. I'm aware of the change in me, but I can't help it.

He had a constant image that plagued him when he thought of the farm and how it used to be, and that was of a drowning man grabbing at everything in sight to survive and keep afloat.

As he leaned forward, he noticed Abigail stood up quickly, put her beer and sandwich down, and stretched her neck looking in Lawrence's direction. At once, Lawrence pulled himself back into the shadows of the forest, the bark from the tree splintered on to the ground. But it was too late because Abigail saw him. "Lawrence, is that you?" Abigail shouted.

All he wanted to do at that point was to run through the woods toward the dirt road and away from the farm. But perhaps there were still courteous manners of a gentleman buried deep in his heart, since he came out from behind the tree.

He waved little by little and without much conviction at Abigail. She started toward him through the newly plowed field, balancing herself on the black furrowed mounds of dirt as she toddled across the field, as if she was a young baby just learning to walk.

Noah and Daniel stood up the instant she started to cross the field. They were at the ready to protect the young girl who was so anxious to reach the other side. Their clenched fists were by their sides, and their focused stares seemed to grab hold of him while he stood motionless.

She finally got to where Lawrence was standing. "How are you, Lawrence?" she asked. All at once, she pulled a leaf off the oak tree and began ripping it in half. It sounded like tearing paper. She looked up at him, between the times that she was dissecting the leaf. Lawrence had to look down at the ground more than once because her eyes were like daggers, questioning him about how and why he changed. He still loved her but could not live with her.

"Okay, I guess," he said. He snapped off a branch from the oak tree, using it like a whip, swishing it through the air, and poking it into the ground and decapitating the head of a tall mushroom. He stared at the mushroom that he had destroyed with the stick as he talked to Abigail. He found it hard to look at her

"What are you doing for money?" she asked.

"Oh, I had a little saved from the time I was in the army," he said. "It's not much, but it keeps me going."

"You look skinnier now than when you came home that day from the war." She looked back toward where Noah and Daniel were standing. "Do you want me to go back and get you a sandwich and beer?"

"No, Abigail, it's all right," he said. "There's some people coming down the road in a little while that I'm getting a ride from."

Abigail reached into the pocket on her skirt and handed Lawrence the ring that he had given her so long ago. "It's hard for me to let this ring go Lawrence, but I know that it belongs to you" She turned her back in a hurry and left without looking at him and talked into the forest as she started to scoot away. "It doesn't mean anything to me anymore."

Lawrence, at the double, threw the stick into the woods and caught Abigail before she could leave. He turned her around and shoved the ring back in her hand. "I want you to keep this to remember me by," he said. Even now, after everything that had happened to them, the touch of her hand sent chills through his spine and made him gasp for breath.

Abigail looked down at the ring, and without hesitation, dropped it on the ground. "I can't take it. Don't you understand?" she said. "It hurts every time I look at it. It reminds me about how things could have been, but weren't." Then she lovingly caressed her belly. "This will always keep us together. We can't throw this away." The baby was growing in her tummy, and it was the culmination of all the good things in their relationship.

Then she ran into the field back toward Noah and Daniel. They were waiting for her in the middle of the pasture. She rushed to Noah and put her face on his chest and cried. He rubbed her back and at the same time stared at Lawrence.

Lawrence bent down and picked off the dead leaves that were hiding the ring and then slipped it on his index finger to look at it one last time. He was bound and determined to throw it into the woods. Although now that he was staring at it, he understood what Abigail meant. The diamonds seemed dull, and the excitement that he saw in it once was gone. Just as he cocked his arm back to throw it away, he changed his mind. He opened up his backpack and dropped it inside.

Lawrence walked back through the woods, crunching through the dead leaves and heading for the road that led out of town. He looked up toward the crest of a hill, and the dust of the road billowed up into the sky, and those friends that he was waiting for were coming down the road. Captain John Webb and his gang of vagabonds descended the crest of the hill, rattling and marching two by two as if they were still in the army. That small covered wagon, that Lawrence was so familiar with, was pulling up the rear of the column. Many nights, Lawrence filled up the baskets overflowing with vegetables and left them on the side of the road, and later, he watched as Webb's soldiers stole them and put them under the white canvas cover.

By now, it was three o'clock in the afternoon, and because it was later in the summer, the sun was lower in the sky so that it wasn't as hot as when he arrived during the beginning of the season. Sitting on the edge of the road, he stole glimpses of the family he once knew and loved. He wondered about the baby and whether it would be a boy or a girl. If he had stayed and their love had survived, he would have hoped for a strong healthy son, but since he was leaving, he hoped that she had a little girl to keep her company.

He sat there by the edge of the road right next to the root cellar, trying not to look directly at it because it brought back a combination of sad and happy memories. And those were times that he'd just as soon forget.

Capt. John Webb stopped in front of Lawrence. "Well, Sunday soldier, ready to go?" He asked.

"I'm ready," Lawrence said. "Only do me one favor, would ya?"

"Yeah what is it?" the captain asked.

"Don't call me, Sunday soldier," Lawrence stared at the officer.

"Okay," he said. "I'll call you Top Rail from now on if you promise not to call me Bugger." His white horse galloped forward as he pulled on the reins to settle him down. "How does that sound? That doesn't sound too uppity, does it? After all, we're all equal here. There's no reason for anybody to get uppity. But just remember this, I'm the boss and whatever I say goes."

"Sounds okay to me," Lawrence said as he got up.

"You'll be as snug as a bug," The captain said. "Where we're going down South, half the county belongs to us. You'll be living like a king."

"Thanks, Captain," Lawrence said. He reached up and shook his gauntlet gloved hand.

Then he walked to the back of the wagon and sat on the tail facing the hill. After all was said and done, Lawrence felt that he had rescued himself from an unhappy life.

They moved down the road away from the farm. He leaned on the rough top of a wooden cask as he watched everything that he knew pass him by; the earthy smell of the rich soil just plowed, the countryside tall with corn, the clapboard farmhouse, and the thing that was the hardest to look at while they moved along the road, the root cellar.

Made in the USA
San Bernardino, CA
12 February 2016